The woman's expression changed as she stared up at him with big eyes. She said slowly, "You don't remember my name?"

There was no point in pretending.

"No. I'm sorry. I mean no disrespect to you or your grandfather. Even if he's trying to kill me." He smiled grimly, and when she didn't return the smile, he sobered and said, "Tell me your name."

There. He'd said *I'm sorry*, which he rarely did.

But she didn't seem particularly impressed. She lifted her chin, her green eyes shooting emerald sparks in the light of the foyer.

"My name is Honora Callahan, my grandfather is Patrick Burke and he thinks you've disrespected both of us. That's why he's on his way here right now with his old hunting rifle, intending to shoot your head off."

"Why would he?"

Honora's pale cheeks seemed to burn. Ducking her head, she glanced down at her belly and mumbled, "You know why."

Nico's heart dropped to the floor, as if somehow his body knew what she was about to say, even though his brain protested it was impossible. "No."

Honora huffed with a flare of her nostrils. "I'm pregnant, Nico. With your baby."

USA TODAY bestselling author **Jennie Lucas**'s parents owned a bookstore, so she grew up surrounded by books, dreaming about faraway lands. A fourth-generation Westerner, she went east at sixteen to boarding school on a scholarship, wandered the world, got married, then finally worked her way through college before happily returning to her hometown. A 2010 RITA® Award finalist and 2005 Golden Heart® Award winner, she lives in Idaho with her husband and children.

Books by Jennie Lucas

Harlequin Presents

Christmas Baby for the Greek
Her Boss's One-Night Baby
Claiming the Virgin's Baby
Penniless and Secretly Pregnant

Conveniently Wed!

Chosen as the Sheikh's Royal Bride

One Night With Consequences

Claiming His Nine-Month Consequence

Secret Heirs and Scandalous Brides

The Secret the Italian Claims
The Heir the Prince Secures
The Baby the Billionaire Demands

Visit the Author Profile page
at Harlequin.com for more titles.

Jennie Lucas

THE ITALIAN'S DOORSTEP SURPRISE

HARLEQUIN
PRESENTS

HARLEQUIN®
PRESENTS®

PLEASE RECYCLE
THIS PRODUCT IS RECYCLABLE

Recycling programs
for this product may
not exist in your area.

ISBN-13: 978-1-335-56790-1

The Italian's Doorstep Surprise

Copyright © 2021 by Jennie Lucas

All rights reserved. No part of this book may be used or reproduced in
any manner whatsoever without written permission except in the case of
brief quotations embodied in critical articles and reviews.

This is a work of fiction. Names, characters, places and incidents
are either the product of the author's imagination or are used fictitiously.
Any resemblance to actual persons, living or dead, businesses,
companies, events or locales is entirely coincidental.

This edition published by arrangement with Harlequin Books S.A.

For questions and comments about the quality of this book,
please contact us at CustomerService@Harlequin.com.

Harlequin Enterprises ULC
22 Adelaide St. West, 40th Floor
Toronto, Ontario M5H 4E3, Canada
www.Harlequin.com

Printed in U.S.A.

THE ITALIAN'S DOORSTEP SURPRISE

CHAPTER ONE

A FIERCE SUMMER storm was raging off the Atlantic coast, pummeling his sprawling oceanfront mansion. Nico Ferraro stared out the open window, his mood as dark as the crashing surf below.

Rain blew inside his study, running down the inside wall to the hardwood floor as bright lightning crackled across the sky. He took another sip of Scotch. Thunder shook the house, rattling the windows. Nico remained unmoving, staring broodingly into the night.

He'd lost the thing that mattered most. All the billions he'd accumulated, his fame, his romantic conquests, meant *nothing*. He'd lost his chance at vengeance, had it ripped from his grasp at the very moment of his triumph.

Nico heard a loud bang from the other side of the house. Not thunder this time. Someone was banging at his front door.

"Please," a woman's voice screamed into the storm. "Please, Mr. Ferraro, you have to let me in."

Nico took another sip of the forty-year-old Scotch. His butler would handle the intruder, assisted by his security team if necessary. He was in no mood to see anyone tonight.

"If you don't, someone will die," she cried.

Now *that* piqued his curiosity. He suddenly wanted to at least hear the woman's story before he tossed her back into the rain. He started to turn from the open window, hesitated, then closed the glass window behind him. He didn't give a damn about this place—just another anonymous fifty-million-dollar Hamptons beach house—but he'd be putting it on the market tomorrow. This estate was useless to him now it could no longer be the scene of his revenge.

Going down the wide hallway to the foyer, he saw three men gathered in a semicircle around the front door. Behind them, Nico saw the smaller shape of a young woman, soaking wet, with her hair plastered to her skin and her clothes stuck to her body...

Nico sucked in his breath as he realized two things.

First, the young woman, beautiful and dark-haired, was pregnant. Beneath the light on the front porch, her white sundress revealed every luscious outline of her body, her full breasts and heavily pregnant belly.

Second, *he knew her.*

"Stop," Nico said, coming forward. "Let her come inside."

His head of security frowned back at him. "I don't know if that's such a good idea, boss. She's been talking wild—"

"Let her in," he cut him off, and his henchman reluctantly stepped aside.

"Thank you, oh, thank you," the young woman cried,

though it was hard to tell if those were tears streaming down her cheeks or rain. She grabbed at Nico's hand urgently. "I was so scared you wouldn't...when I have to tell you—"

"It's all right." Nico tried to remember how to be polite. His skills were a little rusty. "You're safe now, Miss—" Then he realized that he'd forgotten her name, which of course was embarrassing and damnable, since her grandfather was the longtime gardener at his Manhattan penthouse. To cover, he said sharply, "Your hands are like ice." He turned to a bodyguard. "Get her a blanket."

"Of course, Mr. Ferraro."

Her teeth were chattering with cold. "But I have—have to tell you—"

"Whatever it is, it can wait until you're not freezing to death." He started to offer her the half-empty glass of Scotch still in his hand, but then stopped as he remembered pregnant women generally avoided such things. "Perhaps a warm drink?"

"No, really," she croaked, "if you'll just listen—"

Nico turned to his butler. "Find her some hot cocoa."

Sebastian looked rather doubtful. "Cocoa, sir? I'm not sure—"

"Wake the cook," he bit out, and the man scurried off.

It occurred to Nico that his staff had gone to seed. Once, it would have been unnecessary for him to repeat any order—ever. All of his houses, like his international real estate conglomerate, had run like well-oiled machines. Though of course, that was before. How long ago had that been, when Nico had still cared so desperately to make his life appear perfect?

Christmas. It had been Christmas Day. And now it was—

"What day is it?" he barked at his security chief. The man looked at him like he was mad.

"It's the first of July, Mr. Ferraro."

Six months. And he could barely recall any of it, though he'd obviously continued to buy properties and run his company from Rome. He clawed his hand through his dark hair. Was he losing his mind?

"Nico. *Please*."

Hearing his gardener's granddaughter call him by his first name drew Nico's attention as nothing else had. He looked at her.

The young woman gripped his hand, looking up at him pleadingly, and he had a strange stirring of memory. But of what?

He barely knew her. He'd seen her occasionally over the years, of course, as she'd grown up amid the rooftop gardens of Nico's Manhattan penthouse, a few hours from here. She had to be in her midtwenties now. Perhaps he'd said hello once or twice, or wished her happy holidays, that sort of thing, but nothing more. Nothing to warrant her suddenly calling him *Nico*, as if they were friends. As if they were lovers.

He withdrew his hand, folding his arms. "Why are you here? Why have you made such a scene?"

As a bodyguard wrapped a warm blanket over her slender shoulders, she nearly sobbed, "Just *listen*."

"I'm listening," he said. "Tell me."

Her eyes were an uncanny green in her pale complexion, beneath striking dark eyebrows that matched her wild, dark hair. She took a deep breath. "My grandfather is coming here to shoot you."

Nico frowned. "Your grandfather? Why?" He could think of no complaint the gardener might have against him. To his best memory, he hadn't even spoken to the man since before Christmas, when he'd given him exact instructions about the holiday lighting for the pergola and trees on the penthouse terrace. Back when Nico had cared about such things. Back before—

He pushed the thought away. "Is this some kind of joke?"

"Why would I joke about that!"

He saw the terror in her eyes. However ridiculous it sounded, clearly the woman believed her story. So it was either true, or she was having some kind of psychotic breakdown. He could hardly judge her for that, after his six months of near-fugue state as CEO of Ferraro Developments Inc. He knew he'd made multimillion-dollar deals, but he could hardly remember a single one. "Why would he want to kill me, Miss...uh...?"

Damn it. Too late, he remembered *again* that he didn't know. Glaring at the Scotch, which he held entirely to blame, he set the half-empty crystal glass on the hallway table.

The woman's expression changed as she stared up at him with big eyes. She said slowly, "You don't remember my name?"

There was no point in pretending.

"No. I'm sorry. I mean no disrespect to you or your

grandfather. Even if he's trying to kill me." He smiled grimly, and when she didn't return the smile, he sobered and said, "Tell me your name."

There. He'd said *I'm sorry*, which he rarely did.

But she didn't seem particularly impressed. She lifted her chin, her green eyes shooting emerald sparks in the light of the foyer.

"My name is Honora Callahan, my grandfather is Patrick Burke and he thinks you've disrespected both of us. That's why he's on his way here right now with his old hunting rifle, intending to shoot your head off."

Nico almost laughed at the image. He stopped himself just in time. "Why would he?"

She stared at him, her pretty face bewildered. He shifted his feet, growing uncomfortable beneath her searching gaze.

"I'm sure you can guess," she said finally.

He snorted. "How would I know?"

She licked her lips, glancing nervously at Frank Bauer, his security chief, and the other bodyguard still standing by the front door. Both men were pretending not to hear, though they'd moved their hands to their holsters when Honora mentioned her grandfather's rifle.

"Fine," she said. "If that's how you want to play it. But when Granddad gets here, he'll be waving his rifle and shouting crazy threats. Just tell your bodyguards to ignore him. Don't let them hurt him."

"What would you prefer? That I just let your grandfather kill me?" he said acidly. "Burke is a good gardener, but there are limits to what I'll do for employee morale."

"As soon as he gets here, I'll go outside and calm

him down. Just stay in here, and tell your men not to pull out their guns. That's all."

"Hide like a coward in my own home?"

"Oh, for the love of—" Honora stamped her small foot. As she did so, Nico's gaze fell unwillingly on the bounce of her full breasts. He could even see— His mouth went dry. The shape of her hard nipples were clearly visible beneath the wet, thin fabric. "Just stay inside and don't respond." Her voice changed. "Should be easy for you."

There was some criticism there he didn't understand. Forcing his gaze upward, he said, "You still haven't explained why Burke would do this. I haven't spoken to the man for months."

Honora's pale cheeks seemed to burn. Ducking her head, she glanced down at her belly and mumbled, "You know why."

Nico's heart dropped to the floor, as if somehow his body knew what she was about to say, even though his brain protested it was impossible. "No."

Honora huffed with a flare of nostrils. "I'm pregnant, Nico. With your baby."

Lightning flashed, flooding the foyer with brief white light as Honora stared up at Nico's handsome face, her heart pounding. Thunder followed, rattling the windows of the oceanfront mansion. Her whole body was shivering. Not from cold, but from fear.

She'd spent six months dreading the thought of seeing Nico Ferraro again. But she'd never imagined it could be as bad as this.

It shocked her now to remember the schoolgirl crush she'd once had on her grandfather's boss. Her infatuation had lasted throughout her teenage years, all those afternoons she'd helped Granddad after school, or done homework sitting at a bench in the far corner of the penthouse terrace.

She'd been in awe of Nico Ferraro, billionaire real estate tycoon, watching him with big eyes every time he came or went—equally handsome whether wearing a tuxedo with a beautiful woman on his arm as they left for some glamorous ball, or in a black leather jacket, going motorcycle racing; or even in casual khaki shorts, flying off to the Maldives in his private jet. It was a world that Honora couldn't even imagine, even though she'd spent her entire childhood adjacent to it. And now, at thirty-six, he was the most gorgeous man she'd ever seen, a James Bond of the society set.

While Honora often felt invisible. When Granddad was done with his work tending the enormous rooftop garden, treating every plant and flower with loving care, they would head home on the subway to their two-bedroom walk-up in Queens. He'd raised Honora since she was eleven, after her parents had died. He'd been patient, gruffly kind and dutiful in his care of her.

But he saved his true devotion for his plants. Sometimes, Honora had wished she might have been a rhododendron bush, or perhaps a cypress or juniper, in order to get more of his warmth and attention. He seemed to save all of his true love, and most of his conversation, for them. He could chat and coax and croon to his plants in a way he never did to Honora.

But when she felt unloved, she told herself she was lucky her grandfather had taken her in and given her a home. She had no right to ask for more. Patrick Burke had always put duty ahead of all else. Honor was important in their family. So important her mother had named her for it.

That had made it all the more shocking and painful when Honora had had to tell her old-fashioned grandfather that she was pregnant—pregnant and unwed.

She'd known he would find out sooner or later. She'd hidden her pregnancy with loose clothing as long as she could, hoping with increasing desperation that Nico Ferraro would either answer her messages, or return to New York City. But he'd done neither. Which was really all the answer she needed, and it broke her heart.

As spring had turned to summer, it had become increasingly difficult to come up with good excuses to wear oversize hoodies. When New York City suffered its first blast of sticky humid heat in June, she was already so hot in her pregnant state, and their Queens apartment had no air-conditioning. Her grandfather caught her standing in front of the open refrigerator, gasping the cool air in her T-shirt and shorts. His eyes had gone to her belly.

"Oh, no," he'd gasped, and for the first time since her parents' funeral thirteen years before, he'd cried in front of her. Then his tears had turned to rage. "Who is the bastard who did this to you?"

Honora had refused to reveal the father's identity, even to her friends. The chauffeur at the penthouse, Benny Rossini, an Italian American from the Bronx, had offered to marry her, which was very kind. *Too* kind, in fact. She'd thanked him, but couldn't take advantage of their friendship. For a month, she'd held her breath, hoping somehow it would all blow over.

Then today, while she was helping her grandfather tend the rooftop garden, the housekeeper told them that after six months away, Nico Ferraro had finally returned to the US. His private jet had just landed in the Hamptons, a three-hour drive from New York City.

After more than a decade of working for him, Patrick Burke knew his employer's playboy ways. He'd taken one look at Honora's stricken face and dropped his shovel, muttering that he was going to their apartment to get his antique hunting rifle.

Honora had been terrified, imagining Nico Ferraro's security team would take one look at her gray-haired grandfather waving his rifle like a maniac, and shoot the old man down immediately in an act they could reasonably claim was self-defense. Her only hope had been to get there first and reason with her grandfather's employer.

It had taken all of Honora's efforts to talk the older man out of his lunatic plan of jumping on an eastbound train with the big rifle slung openly over his shoulder. "At least have Benny take you," she'd said desperately. "It will be faster than the train."

When her grandfather grudgingly agreed, she'd rushed downstairs to ask the young chauffeur for help with her plan.

Benny had been shocked, then angry, to learn the identity of her baby's father. But he'd recovered quickly and agreed to give her grandfather a ride to the Hamptons in the boss's Bentley, and "accidentally" get lost on the way. He'd added with a nervous laugh, "Just make sure they don't shoot us when we get there."

But her drive had taken longer than she expected. She'd borrowed Benny's personal car, a vintage Beetle, and it had broken down three miles from the house. Terrified of arriving too late, she'd run here. At six months pregnant. In a sleeveless stretchy dress and strappy sandals, in a rain storm with the wind pushing against her every step.

Now, Honora looked between Nico and his bodyguards anxiously. "So you agree? When my grandfather gets here, you'll keep your guns down and let me go out there alone?"

Nico came closer to her in the foyer. "You can't be serious."

She looked up at him, the billionaire playboy she'd once thought so exotic and wonderful. Her hands tightened at her sides. "I told you, this is no joke. Granddad's already on the way, but they're taking the long route—"

"I can't possibly be your baby's father," he interrupted. "I never touched you."

Honora's mouth fell open. Never touched her?

It was one possibility she'd never considered. For him to deny he'd made love to her! As if she were lying about their night together. As if she were some gold digger trying to trap him into marriage under false pretenses!

In February, after she'd discovered she was pregnant, she'd tried to do the right thing and let him know, but he'd ignored all the messages she'd left at his office in Rome and his villa on the Amalfi Coast. Resigned, she'd known she'd have to raise this child alone. If Nico wouldn't take responsibility, so be it. She was a grown-up. She'd known the risks of sex.

But hearing him deny their night together, she realized Nico Ferraro had taken full advantage of her schoolgirl crush. He'd helped himself to her virginity, then meant to toss her and the baby—*his* baby—aside like trash.

It was the final straw.

Fury filled her, rushing like fire all the way to her fingertips and toes, burning her heart to ash.

"How dare you," she said in a low, trembling voice. She clenched her hands into fists. "I have been nothing but honorable—unlike you—and this is how you treat me? By calling me a liar?"

Nico's forehead furrowed, his expression turning perplexed as he stared down at her. "If I'd slept with you, I would remember."

He was tall and broad-shouldered and so handsome, in spite of—or perhaps even because of—his dark hair being uncombed and wild. His tailored white shirt and black trousers were unkempt and wrinkled. He smelled of Scotch and leather and smoke from the fire and rain, everything masculine and untamed. She breathed it in and yearned for him, still, in spite of everything.

She hated herself for that, but not as much as she hated him. She'd never let herself want him again. Never, ever.

"So you don't remember my name and you don't remember our night," she choked out. "How can you be so heartless and cold?"

His dark eyes narrowed as he said acidly, "And when do you claim you conceived this miracle baby?"

"Christmas night."

He snorted. "Christmas—" Then his expression changed. His forehead furrowed, as if straining to remember a half-forgotten dream. For a moment, he looked bewildered. Then he lifted his chin defiantly. "Even if it happened, which I'm not saying it did, how could you be sure I'm the father?"

She looked at him, nearly speechless with anger. "You think I slept with other men the same week?"

"It's the twenty-first century, and you're a free woman…"

"You know I came to your bed a virgin!" She knew his men were listening, but she was too enraged to care. Her cheeks burned. "How dare you!"

Then their eyes widened at the noise of a car outside, and doors slamming.

"Get out here, Ferraro!" she heard her grandfather's voice holler above the wind and rain. "Get out here right now so I can shoot you right between the eyes!"

She looked at the two bodyguards by the door, who'd already put their hands on their holsters.

"Please, don't hurt him," she pleaded. "I told you. I'll go out and talk to him."

The older bodyguard stared at her, then glanced at his boss. She saw Nico Ferraro give him a tiny nod, and she hated him for that. How awful to have to ask him for favors!

"Keep him outside," the head bodyguard said. "If he doesn't shoot at us, we won't shoot back."

"Thank you," Honora said, but fear caught at her throat. How could she guarantee Patrick wouldn't start taking potshots at the house in his current emotional state? Trembling, she hurried to the front door.

Then she suddenly stopped, whirling back to face Nico.

"I'm doing this to protect Granddad, not you," she said. "Personally, I think I'd be happy to see you shot."

And opening the door, she ran out into the dark summer storm, beneath the torrent of rain and howling wind on the wild Atlantic shore.

CHAPTER TWO

PERSONALLY, I THINK I'd be happy to see you shot.

As Honora disappeared out the beach house's front door into the storm, Nico stared after her in shock. Standing in the foyer, he felt his men's gaze on him, before they discreetly turned away. He felt a twist in his solar plexus.

So you don't remember my name and you don't remember our night. How can you be so heartless and cold?

Her scornful words made him feel hollow inside, reminding him of similar words from Lana when he'd called her film set in Paris on Christmas Eve to end their engagement.

You heartless bastard. You never loved me at all, did you? Lana had yelled into the phone.

No, he'd replied shortly. *Sorry.*

Being woken earlier that morning with news of his estranged father's death had felt like being submerged in ice water. Prince Arnaldo Caracciola had dropped dead of a heart attack in Rome, right before he would have been forced to fly to the Hamptons to beg for Nico's mercy.

What point was there in being engaged to a movie star if he couldn't rub the old man's face in it?

After hanging up with Lana, Nico had tried to go to work as if nothing had happened, but he'd found himself shouting at, even firing, several of his most valued employees. "It's Christmas Eve. Go home before you ruin us," his vice president of operations had said quietly, then handed him two sleeping pills. "Get some rest. You look like you haven't slept in days."

It was true; he'd barely slept all week in anticipation of his father's visit. But Nico didn't need sleep. He was fine. Never better. To prove it, he'd gone to his gritty downtown gym and sparred against a former heavyweight boxing champion. Nico had pushed himself in the ring, insulting his bigger, better-skilled opponent, until he'd gotten himself knocked out twice. The second time, when he sat up, he hadn't been able to see anything for nearly three minutes. But as soon as his sight returned, he'd started to get back in the ring.

The owner of the gym would not allow it. "You want to destroy your brain, Mr. Ferraro, go do it somewhere else. I'm not running a morgue. And get a doctor to look at that concussion!"

Doctor. Nico had sneered at the idea, but his head had ached as he walked back the long city blocks to his midtown penthouse.

Late afternoon on Christmas Eve, his home had been deserted, all the employees gone home to spend the holiday with their families. The dark, empty rooms had echoed inside him. He'd reached for a bottle of Scotch, sent to him by a rival congratulating him on his recent acquisition of beachfront land in Rio, which would soon be developed into a world-class hotel. He'd paced all Christmas Eve night, looking out at the city lights, his soul howling with fury.

He didn't remember much after that. He'd started to hallucinate and imagine things. At some point, he must have taken the two sleeping pills and washed them down with Scotch, because when his housekeeper arrived early the day after Christmas, she'd found him collapsed in the hallway with a smashed bottle of Scotch on the floor. Alarmed, she'd called an ambulance.

Nico had woken up in the hospital to see his doctor standing over him with worried eyes. "You need to take better care of yourself, Mr. Ferraro. You've had a severe concussion, which was not helped by alcohol and sleeping pills." He'd paused delicately. "Perhaps you'd find it beneficial to talk to someone. Or I could recommend a residential facility that would help you rest and work through whatever you're—"

"I'm fine," Nico had said, detaching himself from the monitors. Against medical advice, he'd checked himself out of the hospital and rolled onto his private jet, just in time to make it to the old man's funeral in Rome.

His father, who'd denied him everything all his life, couldn't stop him from doing it, now he was dead. Nico had had the last word. But as his evil stepmother glared at him with tearful, accusatory eyes over the grave, Nico had felt otherwise. He'd felt heartsick that wintry day in Rome, as if his father had won, contriving to die of a heart attack just when Nico finally had him by the throat.

Now, Arnaldo would never be forced to admit that his abandoned son had surpassed him, or to say that he was desperately sorry for seducing his maid, Nico's mother, then tossing her out like trash. The married prince had known Maria Ferraro was pregnant, but he'd still refused to take responsibility. He'd left her and Nico to starve. The man deserved to be punished for—

Personally, I think I'd be happy to see you shot.

Nico sucked in his breath. Was it possible that he was doing the same thing as the man he'd despised?

Could Nico have fathered a child with—well, not a maid, but with his gardener's granddaughter? Could Honora Callahan be telling the truth?

No. He would remember!

He'd never had an affair with an employee. He preferred the women he slept with to have power that matched his own. His mistresses before Lana Lee had been supermodels. Heiresses. A chemist. A makeup millionaire. They were women who wanted hot sex, who wanted to see and be seen, but who wouldn't demand emotional intimacy he couldn't give. For the entirety of their six-month engagement, he'd never felt emotionally close to Lana; he'd assumed she preferred it that way, too.

The idea of anyone sacrificing their own self-interest for the sake of someone else seemed like total insanity to Nico.

Like when Patrick Burke became guardian to his orphaned granddaughter thirteen years before. Nico had thought it was sheer lunacy for an elderly widower to raise an eleven-year-old child. But it didn't affect the man's work, so Nico had never said so. He had no right to an opinion.

But the old man sure seemed to have an opinion about his employer, coming here with a hunting rifle.

Going to the window, Nico looked past the silk curtains. In the dim light from the windows, he saw Honora talking to her grandfather some distance from the house, beneath the lightning and rain. There was another dark figure hovering nearby. What the hell? Was that his chauffeur, who'd apparently driven the murderous old gardener here to kill him, in Nico's own Bentley?

He saw the old man waving the rifle around, seeming to point it toward the house. He couldn't hear his words.

There was another flash of lightning, and he saw Honora's pleading face before she turned away, trying to block her grandfather from approaching the house.

Patrick Burke seemed very sure that Nico was the father. Honora had seemed so, too. *You know I came to your bed a virgin.*

But he would remember sleeping with her, wouldn't he? Yes, he'd slept with many beautiful women, and some people called him a player. But even with a bad concussion, even hallucinating from insomnia, even on sleeping pills washed down with Scotch, he'd remember—

Her long, dark hair spread across his pillow. Her emerald eyes glowing up at him as she whispered, *I can't believe this is happening...* The softness of her skin as he slowly stroked down her naked body, cupping her breasts, then moving down farther still, as he lowered his mouth to taste her sweetness...

Oh, my God. Nico's eyes went wide.

Turning abruptly from the window, he pushed open the door and went out into the dark, wind and rain.

Behind him, he heard Bauer shouting, "Sir?"

The Bentley was parked in the circular driveway, with his chauffeur standing behind it. Nico went straight to where the old man stood with Honora.

The old gardener sobered when he saw Nico. He quit waving the rifle around, even as he lifted his chin defiantly.

"You think you can just take whatever you want, Mr. Ferraro?" His voice broke. "Even seduce an innocent girl, and then toss her callously aside, when she's pregnant with your child?"

"I didn't know," Nico ground out. "She never told me."

Her eyes narrowed. "I tried."

"Well, now that you know," Patrick Burke said pointedly, "what are you going to do about it?"

Honora nervously placed herself between the two men, as if she were afraid of what they might do. "I don't need him to do anything, Granddad. He made it clear he's not interested in being a father. I can raise my baby alone."

Not interested in being a father. It was jarring. He had a sudden flash of a memory of his own mother holding him tight when he was a boy, and they were evicted from their tiny apartment outside Rome.

Why won't your father pay for you? Why doesn't he want you? How does he expect me to do this on my own?

Now, Nico felt oddly suspended in time as the storm pelted him with rain and lightning flashed across the wide dark sky. In the distance, he could hear the roar of the ocean against the shore.

For six months, he'd been lost, even to himself, after the failure of a lifetime's worth of plans. Just when ultimate triumph had been within his grasp, he'd lost his last chance at victory. His father was dead, and would never recognize Nico's right to exist, much less claim him as his son.

Nico couldn't inflict the same pain his father had. He could claim his own child.

If this baby was his, he had the opportunity to be better than his father ever was.

Nico could never inherit the title of prince, or the aristocratic Caracciola name. But he could sire his own dynasty. Build his own legacy. And make sure that his own children never felt as he had—rejected, adrift, alone.

"You *will* do something about it," Patrick Burke told him fiercely, his whiskers shaking beneath the rain as he shook his rifle in Nico's direction. "You'll take responsibility for what you've done! Or meet the short end of this stick!"

Reaching out, Nico yanked the rifle away in a swift, easy movement. For a moment, the old man stared at him, shocked and outraged.

Backing up a step, Nico held the rifle almost casually, pointing it upward. "I take your point, Mr. Burke. I believe we can come to some arrangement."

"Arrangement?" Those bushy gray eyebrows shook. But it wasn't just his eyebrows, Nico realized. The man's hands were shaking, as well. He was upset. And why shouldn't he be if he truly believed his boss had coldly taken Honora's virginity and then refused to take responsibility? "What kind of arrangement?"

Nico looked at Honora, who was watching with big eyes as rain fell, all of them so wet they might as well have been swimming in the sea. "Why don't you come inside where it's warm, and we can discuss it."

The old man scowled. "If you think my granddaughter will ever accept a payoff…"

"No. If she is pregnant with my baby, there can be only one answer." Lifting his chin, Nico looked straight at Honora's lovely, worried face. "I will marry her."

Honora's jaw fell open. She felt dizzy.

Behind her, Benny Rossini, the young chauffeur, said harshly, "You don't have to do that, Mr. Ferraro…"

But her grandfather was staring only at Nico. "Do you give me your word, sir?"

Nico Ferraro's handsome face was deadly serious. "I do."

"Well, then!" Her grandfather was suddenly beaming. A flash of lightning crackled in a sizzling line above them, cracking the sky. He came toward Nico, holding out his hand. "Welcome to the family."

"Thank you," said Nico, shaking his hand gravely, still holding the rifle upright with the other.

And just like that, it seemed, Honora's fate was sealed.

Was she losing her mind?

"What century are we living in?" she said incredulously. She looked at Nico. "I'm not going to marry you!"

Her grandfather, whom she'd always trusted and obeyed, turned to her almost chidingly. "That's no way to talk to your husband, little one…"

"My *future* husband. Which he isn't!"

Patrick waved his hand airily. "You two kids have a lot to talk about." Turning to Benny, he said, "We should give the happy couple time to discuss wedding plans."

"Wedding plans?" she sputtered.

"But there's no reason to remain out here in the cold and rain." Nico nodded toward his sprawling Hamptons beach house. "Come inside."

As Benny started to step forward, Patrick stopped him with his hand on his arm.

"No." Her grandfather's shoulders sagged in his old coat, as if he'd just aged twenty years in five seconds. "I'm exhausted, as only an old man can be. Please, Benny." He looked at the young chauffeur plaintively. "Just take me home."

Honora looked at her grandfather sharply. Other than a touch of arthritis, Patrick Burke was more energetic than some men half his age. Was he up to something? Or had the worry of her unwed pregnancy truly exhausted him?

"All right," Benny said grudgingly. Turning to Honora, he said, "You coming?"

She bit her lip. She was grateful the young driver had helped her keep Granddad from harm, but she was afraid Benny felt more for her than friendship. And she'd never love him back, no matter how many times he offered to run down to the local bodega to buy her ice cream and pickles. No matter how many times he tenderly offered to marry her and be the father her baby "obviously needed."

It annoyed her. Why was it that everyone seemed to think that just because Honora was pregnant, she was desperate for a husband? They didn't seem to realize, as Nico had said earlier, that it was the twenty-first century!

But at least Benny's proposal had been real. Unlike Nico's. Setting her jaw, she tossed a glare at her baby's father.

"Please take Granddad home, Benny. I want to stay and have a little chat with my *future husband* here."

"Honora," her grandfather said quietly, "be nice."

Be nice.

He rarely spoke those words to her, but they always made her shrink back in shame. Had she been unkind? Rude? Selfish? Had she acted in a way that meant she didn't deserve to be loved—didn't even deserve a home? *Be nice* made her try harder to be good, to be helpful, to be no trouble to anyone.

But this time, the unfairness of it made her catch her breath.

Turning in amazement, she glanced pointedly at the old hunting rifle. Patrick had the grace to blush.

"That's different," he said with dignity. "I was just doing a grandfather's duty."

"You're right. We do have a great deal to discuss." Nico gave her a calm smile. "It's late. I'll take you back to the city first thing in the morning."

"Honora?" Benny demanded.

"Go. I'll be fine." Her eyes narrowed. But she wouldn't say as much for Nico.

Nico gave the rifle back to Patrick, who pointed the muzzle at the ground, looking a little embarrassed.

"Oh, Benny." She suddenly remembered. "Your car broke down a few miles up the road."

"Then how did you get here?"

She shrugged beneath the rain. "I ran." She felt, rather than saw, all three men look at her belly, as if judging her ability to run by her condition, and felt irritated. "It was fine. I'm fine."

"You need to be careful," her grandfather began.

"I'm so sorry," Benny said at the same time. "I thought the engine was okay. I'll have it towed tomorrow."

"My men will handle it," Nico said coolly. "I'll have it repaired and brought to you. No charge of course." He glanced at Honora. "Not when your car brought me such happy news."

Benny ground his teeth into a smile at his boss. Then he turned and said reluctantly, "All right, Mr. Burke. I'll take you home."

"Great." Her grandfather turned and leaped back to the Bentley like a teenager running a hundred-meter dash. Honora's throat caught. So much for him being exhausted. She'd spent her whole life trying to be helpful and sweet and no trouble at all, either to her parents or, later, to her grandfather. Was she really such a burden that Granddad seemed so eager to be free of her?

"And this time, take the interstate," the old man called to Benny. "I have no idea where you thought you were going, driving in loops all over Long Island. I'd expect a chauffeur to have a better sense of direction."

Honora watched as the Bentley pulled away into the stormy night. Then she exhaled and turned to her grandfather's boss.

"You have some nerve."

"Say it inside."

Taking her hand, Nico pulled her toward the house, out of the rain. She felt the warmth and strength of his palm against hers, and even hating him as she did, she shivered a little.

Once inside the grand foyer, as the front door closed behind them with a bang, she felt how much warmer it was, and realized that she was soaked to the bone.

"You need to warm up." He glanced at his butler. "Where's her cocoa?"

She had her anger to keep her warm. "I don't need cocoa."

"Cook had to send out for chocolate, sir. She's warming the milk—"

"Tell her to hurry," Nico said. "But first take Miss Callahan upstairs to the rose room. She'll be staying the night."

Was no one listening to her? Honora lifted her chin. "I have not agreed to—"

"Make sure she has everything she might require for her stay," Nico said, ignoring her as he seemed to ignore anything contrary to his will.

"Of course," the butler intoned. "Miss Callahan, if you'll just come this way…"

"I can't sleep here," she said to Nico. "Unless you expect me to sleep naked."

All four men in the foyer stared at her, startled. It took several seconds before any of them recovered. The butler was the first to clear his throat.

"We have ladies' pajamas," he ventured, "clean and never worn that I believe might fit." Honora looked incredulously at Nico. Ladies' pajamas! Did he bring lovers here on a regular basis? The butler continued, "And if you'll just leave your clothes outside your door tonight, they'll be washed, pressed and ready in the morning."

"You don't need to fuss over me," she told the butler. "My grandfather's a member of staff. I can catch a train back later tonight."

Nico said sharply, "Don't be ridiculous. You're cold and wet, and clearly you've had a difficult night. If you're the mother of my unborn child—"

"If?"

"Then I must insist you take care of yourself. Go take a hot shower. We can speak after you're warm."

"You'd like that, wouldn't you?"

"Yes," Nico growled, moving closer. "I would. And if you don't go with Sebastian right now, I'll take you upstairs myself."

Honora's eyes went wide at his threat. The two

of them, alone in a bedroom? Even if he couldn't re-member their night together, she did. Every moment of shocking pleasure would be forever burned on her skin, on her body, on her soul. Even if the secret sen-sual dreams she still had of him made her hate herself. She'd never forget. Especially not now that she was car-rying his baby inside her.

"Fine," she bit out. Following the butler, Sebas-tian—she wondered whether it was his first name, or his last—she went up the sweeping staircase and was escorted to an elegant, feminine room all in pink, where she found a brand-new, freshly laundered white silk nightgown and robe, as well as men's pajamas and a white cotton bathrobe. The soaps and shampoos were Italian and imported.

This guest room had been meant for someone, she thought. But who?

The shower warmed her up and made her feel human again, as well as sleepy and comfortable. Suddenly, the idea of sleeping here rather than shivering on a rattling, cold train through all hours of the night seemed like an excellent plan. Which made her mad. She didn't want Nico to make her feel good. She hated him for what he'd done, for what he was continuing to do.

I will marry her, indeed! She ground her teeth. Say-ing that to her *grandfather*! How could he!

Going downstairs in the soft silk nightgown and matching white robe that she was amazed fit her preg-nant body so well, she found Nico in the grand living room off the stairs, beneath the wall of tall, curved windows overlooking the dark night. He was sitting in a sleek sofa beside a roaring fire.

For a moment, Honora hesitated, her gaze tracing over him unwillingly. It looked as if he'd had a shower, too. His dark hair was just long enough to be wavy, which looked impossibly sexy and Italian over his high chiseled cheekbones. He'd changed into comfortable clothes. A thin white T-shirt clung to his hard-muscled torso and low-slung sweatpants hung over his power-ful thighs. His aquiline profile was facing the fire. His mood seemed pensive, even sad. She felt instinctive sympathy rise inside her.

She fought it with fury. Nicolo Ferraro feel sad? Not about anything but a dip in the stock market or a sud-den drop in commercial rental rates!

Still. Best to get this conversation over with so they could move on with their lives. And she could go to bed. Striding forward purposefully, Honora sat next to him on the sofa. She was careful not to touch him.

"Look, I know you were trying to help," she started, "but you've only made it worse with your lie."

Nico looked at her, his handsome face bemused. "What lie?"

"Telling Granddad you wanted to marry me. Sure, that solved today's problem, but long term it will be ten times worse. Do you think he won't notice when you swan through the penthouse a week from now with some Instagram model?"

"I wasn't lying," he said, sipping a glass of amber liquid. "I'm going to marry you."

She stared at him. "You can't be serious."

"Why?" He turned when Sebastian brought in a white ceramic mug on a silver tray.

"I apologize it took so long, Mr. Ferraro. Apparently the grocer had to be awoken to find and deliver the chocolate."

"It's fine." But as Nico reached for the mug, he drew his hand back in irritation. "But it's cold."

The man bit his lip. "It was ready some moments ago, but as the young lady was upstairs—"

"Make another," Nico said impatiently, leaving the mug on the tray.

"I don't actually like cocoa," Honora said.

Nico turned to her. "What do you want? Herbal tea? Hot apple cider?"

She could only imagine how much trouble that would make for the poor cook. Poor woman would probably be forced to go out and pick apples in the rain. "I want you to leave me alone."

He said to his butler, "Herbal tea. With organic milk." Turning to Honora, he confided, "Calcium is good for the baby."

"Oh, is it now." As if she hadn't just spent the last six months reading every baby book and going to doctor's appointments, while he'd only known about it for, like, ten minutes and already considered himself the expert. She couldn't keep the sarcasm out of her voice as she added, "Tell me more about what my baby needs."

As the butler disappeared, Nico looked at her calmly. The firelight flickered over the hard, handsome planes of his face and the five-o'clock shadow over his square jawline. "A father, for a start. Why didn't you tell me?"

"I did! I told you that I tried. I sent multiple messages to your office in Rome in February."

"Saying you were pregnant?"

"Just saying it was personal, urgently asking you to return my call."

He stroked his chin. "I don't answer desperate messages from women I don't know. Since I didn't remember our night together, or your name…"

Irritated, she set her jaw. "I also left messages with the housekeeper at your new villa, since I heard you'd sold your apartment in Rome. I asked you to call me back as soon as you arrived."

"The Amalfi Coast is hours from Rome. I never stayed there. I slept at the office."

"What?" That explained why Luisa had sounded so doubtful every time Honora called.

"I have a sofa in my private office. A shower. There was no need for me to leave."

"You slept at the office? For six months?"

"I was working," he bit out. His handsome face was full of shadows. "I was fine."

It sounded awful. When had Nico become a workaholic without a soul? He'd always been intensely focused on work, but in the past, he'd at least found *some* time for fun, whether that meant extreme sports or getting himself engaged to world-famous movie star Lana Lee.

Honora told herself she didn't care. The state of his soul wasn't her problem. "The point is, I did try to tell you. When I never heard a response, I realized you weren't interested in anything I might say to you. So I decided to raise this baby on my own."

His eyes narrowed. "Now that I know, I will give you and the baby everything. Including my name."

"It's not necessary. We're good."

"Good? Good how?"

It was a question Honora had often asked herself in the middle of the night when she couldn't sleep for worrying. Her cheeks went hot. "I have a job."

"Doing what?"

"I work in a flower shop. People need flowers," she added defensively at his incredulous look.

"I'm sure they do, but I can't imagine it's enough to support you and the baby."

"I'm also working my way through community college."

"Studying what?"

She looked at the floor. "General education courses." It was a sore point. Honora still hadn't figured out what she wanted to do as a long-term career. She'd been unable to convince herself to study something she hated, just because it would pay, as her accountant friend Emmie had. "I'll figure something out."

Nico let that pass. "Does your current job even have maternity leave? Benefits?"

Honora bit her lip. Her boss, Phyllis Kowalczyk, was a retiree with few employees. The flower shop seemed more like a labor of love than a growing, profitable business. "Um. I'm not sure…"

"You're probably still living with your grandfather."

Guilt flashed through her. As if she needed to be reminded that she already felt like a burden to him. "So?"

"You deserve more." He lifted an arrogant dark eyebrow. "I will take care of you and the baby."

His tone got her hackles up. "No, thanks."

"Why? Are you in love with someone else? Rossini?"

"Benny?" Frowning, she shook her head. "We're friends."

He relaxed. "Well, then. Shall we say next week for the ceremony?"

Ceremony? "But I don't love you!"

He shrugged. "*Love*. A momentary feeling that makes people do things they regret once the madness passes. A make-believe notion. An illusion. I'm grateful that I'm immune."

Honora stared at him. Was there no getting through?

"I'm not going to marry you." She enunciated the words, trying to drive them into his arrogant brain. "I'd be a horrible wife for you. And *you*...you would be a disaster."

Nico looked at her, his handsome face impassive.

"Why did you sleep with me, then?" he asked quietly. "Was it so horrible? Was it such a disaster?"

Everything she'd been about to say got caught in her throat. *Yes*, she wanted to tell him, *it was a mistake*. But then that would mean her baby was a mistake, and she wasn't. She was precious.

As for that night... Honora remembered the sparkling Christmas lights glowing every color in the frosty night. The scent of pine from the enormous, decorated tree in the penthouse with two-story windows overlooking all of glittering Manhattan.

And Nico, taking her in his powerful arms. The taste of his kiss, sweetness and Scotch, savage and tender all at once. The feel of his body against hers as he'd made her feel pleasure she'd never imagined.

Honora couldn't lie. She took a deep breath. Looking up at him with tears in her eyes, she whispered, "It was the most beautiful night of my life."

CHAPTER THREE

NICO STARED AT HER in the enormous living room, as the warm fire flickered over her lovely face. Outside, he could still dimly hear the wind and rain and the crashing surf. But in his heart, something tight...loosened, and he could breathe again.

"I wish I could remember." His voice was quiet. "As you can."

Honora gave a smile that seemed sad. "And I wish I could forget. Like you."

He looked at her sitting at the other end of the sleek new sofa, wrapped in the white robe. Her dark hair was still damp, tumbling over her shoulders in a way that was much too sexy for comfort. And if she leaned forward, the robe fell open a little, revealing the neckline of the silk nightgown. Modest as it was, her full, pregnancy breasts strained against the silk. Swallowing hard, he forced himself to look only at her eyes. "If it was the best night of your life, why do you want to forget?"

She looked away. "Because...because it hurts to remember what a fool I was. Imagining I was in love with you. Imagining I even *knew* you."

Nico had sudden disjointed flashes of memory, the feeling of holding her in his arms in the penthouse, kissing her passionately against the window with all of Manhattan's skyscrapers sparkling behind her. Taking off her clothes piece by piece, pulling her down on the soft rug beneath the Christmas tree… Later, he'd thought it was a hallucination, a dream of a sexy dark-haired woman whose exact features he could not recall.

I love you, Nico. I wasn't brave enough to say it before. I love you.

Abruptly, he stood up and went to the wet bar. Pulling a crystal lowball glass from the shelf, he dumped in two cubes of ice. He opened a new bottle of Scotch and poured a generous amount over the ice. He swallowed the first sweet sip, trying to control the pounding of his heart.

Lifting her gaze, Honora said quietly, "You were drunk the night we slept together, weren't you? That's why you don't remember. You were drunk."

A thousand excuses poured into his mind. Evade, deny, don't say anything that could be used against him, either in a court of law or in the much rougher court of public opinion.

But as Nico looked into her face, he thought how easy it would have been for her to lie and say that their night together had been awful, a tragedy, that she regretted it and hated him. She'd certainly proven that she had no problems insulting him to his face. But she hadn't.

She'd been brave enough to tell the truth. He could

at least tell her something that wasn't a lie. "It's more complicated than that."

"Tell me."

"I had…some problems. I hadn't been sleeping, and I took pills for a…bad headache. Janet—" that was the penthouse's housekeeper "—found me collapsed on the hallway floor the next morning and called an ambulance," he said bluntly. "You didn't know?"

She shook her head, wide-eyed.

"Good." He was relieved his housekeeper was discreet and not spreading rumors. He felt foolish enough to imagine himself insensate and drooling on the floor when she'd discovered him. It was horrible to imagine he'd made a fool of himself in front of Honora, slurring his words or stumbling around. "I didn't seem…off to you on Christmas Day?"

"You did seem a little…different. You had some bruises, but you laughed it off and said it was just from boxing in the gym."

So he'd told her that much. "It was."

"I knew you'd broken up with your fiancée the day before." She looked at her hands. "I thought I was so lucky, like you'd suddenly realized I was the one you'd wanted all that time." She looked up. "But I was just a booty call, wasn't I? No, worse, I was a booty *delivery*—I just happened to be there."

It hadn't been breaking up with Lana that had crushed him, but losing the dream of revenge that had poured rocket fuel on his whole life. But he could hardly explain, since only one other living person even knew that Prince Arnaldo Caracciola was his biological father. "I'm sorry."

It was the second time he'd said that to her. It was starting to become a habit.

"Me too." Her eyes met his. "I was so sure I loved you. Then, when you disappeared and never even bothered to contact me again, I realized I'd loved a dream."

Nico hated imagining that he'd caused her pain. He didn't know her very well, but the more he knew, the more he thought that she was like her name: honorable. And also loving and kind. Perhaps too much of those things—because how could she ever have looked at Nico, with his tattered soul and empty heart, and imagined in her innocence that she saw something worthy of love?

"Honora," he said in a low voice, "you must know I never meant to—"

He stopped as the butler came in with a mug on a tray.

"Your tea with milk, madam." He sounded faintly disapproving. "We had to send out for organic milk."

Honora's cheeks turned rosy. "I never asked for—" But when the butler continued to hold out the tray, she took the mug with a sigh. "Thank you. I'm sorry I was so much trouble."

"My pleasure, madam." The butler turned toward Nico. "Anything else, sir?"

"No, nothing," he said coolly, not even looking at him.

After the butler left, she took a small exploratory sip. She looked very cozy on the sofa in the flickering shadows of firelight. Still holding his barely tasted Scotch, he went to sit beside her, a little closer than he'd been before.

After another sip of tea, she looked at him. "It's not bad." She tilted her head. "You aren't very worried about your employees' feelings though, are you?"

"What?" Frowning, he said, "They should be worried about *mine*. It seems ridiculous that we'd be out of milk and chocolate, even if I arrived with no warning."

"Do you usually require organic milk and cocoa powder?"

"No, I never touch the stuff." Her lips lifted on the edges, and he realized her point. So he changed the subject. "I didn't like Sebastian's tone with you."

"Since your bodyguards didn't shoot Granddad, I'm happy for your staff to talk in any tone they want." She tilted her head. "Two bodyguards? Is that really necessary? Is there so much crime in the Hamptons?"

"Any self-made man makes enemies," he said shortly. He didn't want to talk about his employees. He moved toward her on the sofa. "So is that why you don't want to marry me? Because I hurt you when I ignored your messages in Rome? I told you, I had no idea—"

"It's not just that," she said in a small voice. Looking down at the mug in her hands, she bit her full, tender pink lower lip. "You're very rich, Nico," she said finally. "Incredibly powerful. And as handsome as the devil himself."

He knew she didn't mean it as a compliment. "But?"

She looked up. "A relationship has to be more. There has to be respect on both sides. Trust."

"And you think you can't trust me."

Honora shook her head. "We have nothing in common."

He looked at her baby bump.

"Obviously that's not true," he said quietly.

She looked sad. "It's not enough."

What she meant was that *Nico* wasn't enough. And how could he argue with that? He had secrets he would never share. Not with anyone. Especially not her.

Because he suddenly realized he cared about her opinion. The thought shocked him. For the first time since Christmas, he wanted to make an effort. He wanted someone to think better of him.

Looking up, she threw him a tentative smile. "I'm curious. Why do you believe me now about the baby? What changed your mind enough to make you suddenly propose to me?" She shook her head. "I thought you were just trying to placate Granddad. But you actually meant it."

"Yes."

"Without so much as a DNA test?"

How could he explain what he himself did not really understand? Had he decided to believe her out of pure instinct, based on his perception of her honor and honesty? Or was it because, after months of working sixteen-hour days on projects he could not remember and barely cared about, he grasped at one final chance to prove to his dead father, and himself, that he was a better man than Arnaldo ever was?

And what do you know about being a father? a voice said mockingly inside him. He squelched it coldly. He'd show up, for a start. That would be more than Arnaldo had ever done. "I suppose I could ask for a paternity test…"

"After the baby is born, I guess." She seemed doubtful. "But I'm not going to risk my baby's health on an intrusive test just to convince you."

"After," he agreed. He wasn't worried about it. He already knew this baby was his, in the same way he knew when an undeveloped plot of land would pay off. In the same way he'd known since he was twelve years old that someday he'd *be* somebody, that he'd put his boot against the throat of the world to prove his worth.

Honora tilted her head. In an uncertain voice, she said, "You really want to be a father?"

"How much clearer can I make it?"

"You've never shown the slightest interest in children."

"I've never had one."

"Or commitment. Except for Lana Lee. And even with her, you were only together a few months…"

He gave a crooked half smile. "You were paying attention?"

Her cheeks burned. She set down her empty mug on the end table. "You always changed the color of roses you wished grown in the greenhouse based on the woman you were giving them to."

She must have helped her grandfather with the gardening more than he'd realized. It was strange to realize that Honora knew him so well, when he knew so little about her. Strange and disconcerting.

Her tender pink lips twisted. "Are you still in love with Lana?"

Nico wondered what it had cost her pride to ask. With anyone else, he might have refused to answer. But he didn't want to do that. Not when the stakes were so high. And anyway, in this case honesty cost him nothing. "No."

"You can tell me the truth. You must have been heart-broken on Christmas Day, otherwise you wouldn't have been drinking so much."

"I told you, it wasn't my drinking that was the problem. At least—" he flinched a little "—not the only problem."

"Right. You also said you hadn't slept in days and took pills for a horrible headache." She tilted her head. "Sure sounds like a broken heart to me."

"The headache was a concussion from picking a fight with a world heavyweight champ at my gym."

Her pretty face was tranquil. "And that level of pure stupidity could only come from a broken heart."

He shook his head with a snort. "I told you, I don't *do* love. So my heart can never be broken, as you so romantically describe." He took a deep breath, then said, "I'd just found out my father died."

It was the first time he'd said those words to anyone.

Honora's eyes went wide. "Oh, no! I'm so sorry." Reaching out, she put her hand on his, seeking to offer comfort. "I didn't know…"

"We were…estranged." That was the understatement of the century. "But I'd expected my father and his wife to come here the day after Christmas."

"So that's why you had my room ready for guests." Her eyes glistened with sympathetic tears. "How awful. I'm so sorry. I… I know what it feels like to lose your parents. I know how badly it hurts."

"Yes," he said, feeling like a fraud. Honora had clearly loved her own parents. If she knew the real reason he was upset…

Honora glanced at his half-empty glass of Scotch. "But you have to learn other ways to deal with your grief. Or it will eat you alive."

Her hand felt soft and warm on his own. She was so close on the sofa, almost touching him, that he could feel the warmth of her, the heat of her body. She was so beautiful, with those haunting green eyes, and the massive amounts of damp, dark hair tumbling over her shoulders, leaving traces of wet on the white silk robe that barely contained her lush body. As he looked down at her, he felt an unbearable surge of desire. His gaze fell to her mouth.

Her lips parted as he heard her intake of breath.

Nico didn't think. He didn't hesitate.

Cupping her face with both his hands, he lowered his head and kissed her.

Honora's lips parted in a gasp as his mouth seared hers.

His kiss was sweet, so sweet. For a moment, in her surprise, she was lost in a sensual haze. Her hands moved to his hair.

His embrace, which had started out so exploratory, so tender, turned hungry. He reached inside her silk robe—

Wrenching away, she stood up from the sofa. "No."

Nico looked up at her. His hair was tousled, his dark eyes hazy with desire. His forehead furrowed as he stared up at her, as if he didn't understand.

But Honora still remembered how lonely and cheap she'd felt after their night together, when she'd discovered Nico had left for Italy without a word. When she'd discovered she was pregnant. When he ignored her messages.

She had changed her life forever in that one night, just by loving the wrong man. She wouldn't make that mistake again.

"Maybe you're accustomed to women falling at your feet," she said coldly, wrapping the robe around her pregnant belly more firmly, "but I won't be one of them. So if you were trying to lure me into bed by pretending to have a heart, don't bother."

She started to turn to go, but as she did, he said in a low voice, "Don't make it seem like I'm using you. I felt how you just kissed me. You want me, too."

Honora could hardly deny it. She ground her teeth. "Even if that's true, I'm not going to do anything about it. You're not the right man for me."

He didn't move from the sofa. "How do you know?" He lifted his chin. "From the moment I learned you were pregnant, I've tried to take responsibility. I proposed marriage. I made you tea."

"And am I supposed to be grateful?"

"I even told you about my father, something I've shared with no one else on earth." His dark eyes glittered in the flickering firelight of the salon. "What more do you want?"

What more did Honora want?

So many things.

She wanted to be the naive twenty-four-year-old she'd been, with her whole life ahead of her and no need to rush to make plans or decisions. She wanted her grandfather to be happy, and to know that she wasn't a burden to him. She wanted to have a college degree and a lucrative career so she could get her own apartment and provide for her baby and pay her bills without worry.

She wanted to fall in love, really in love, with a man who would love her back with his whole heart. She wanted him to propose because he loved her—not out of sense of duty, which was the unromantic reason her own parents had married, and her grandparents, too.

She wanted a joyous wedding attended by their friends and family, who were all ecstatic because they thought the two of them so perfect together. She wanted a happy family for her daughter in a real home, where she'd never feel like Honora had, like a burden no one truly wanted.

With an intake of breath, she whispered, "I want more than you can ever give me."

Never taking his eyes from her, Nico rose to his feet. He towered over her, making her feel delicate and petite, even at six months pregnant. He stood close, without touching her, and as their eyes met in the flickering red shadows, he made her feel so *alive*. He said in a low voice, "You don't know that."

"Wrong. I do." Her teeth were chattering with the effort it took not to lean forward, to be closer to him, to be embraced in the circle of his warmth and power.

"Let me tell you what I know, *cara*," he said softly. His hand tucked back a long tendril of her hair and she nearly shuddered, just from that small touch. "I know that I've felt half dead for the last six months, and getting the news you've given me today has brought me back to life."

"It's just an emotion. Like you said." She tried to smile. "Don't let a fleeting emotion make you do something you'll regret…"

Nico pulled her into his arms, his dark eyes piercing her soul.

"I want to be your husband. And I am our baby's father. That is not emotion. That is fact." He nuzzled her as he whispered, "And I want to be your lover…"

With his arms around her, it was so hard to resist. Her body was already galloping ahead, coming up with a million excuses that would lead to another spectacular night upstairs, and the promise of a lifetime more.

And yet… That was the mistake she'd made at Christmas. Letting her body and heart do the thinking, instead of her brain. And that one simple choice had ended so many of her dreams.

Honora had to be smart now. She wasn't an innocent, careless girl anymore. In less than three months, she'd be a mother. At twenty-four, she didn't feel remotely ready for such an enormous responsibility. But it was hers regardless.

She pulled away from him.

"We both know you're not the type to commit to forever," she said quietly. At his startled look, she shook her head ruefully. "I don't mean any insult. But whatever you might be thinking now, we both know who you are. You're a player, Nico. You'll never settle down—especially with a woman you don't love."

"Perhaps this is my moment," Nico said. "Finding out I'm going to be a father has changed me. That could change anyone."

"But it won't."

His expression hardened. "Why else would I marry you, except out of duty?"

"For love." She felt an ache in her throat. How different it would have been if he'd loved her! If they'd already been married. How happy they might have been together, expecting their first baby!

"Then marry me for love," he said. "You said you loved me the night we conceived our baby."

How could he throw that in her face? Swallowing hard, she shook her head. "Those were the romantic dreams of a girl. Growing up, I watched you from a distance and you seemed so handsome and powerful, building skyscrapers and traveling the world. But that wasn't love."

"What was it, then?"

"Illusion."

"Fine." He set his jaw. "How about our child? Doesn't he or she need a father?"

"Why does everyone keep saying that?"

"They keep saying it because it's true," he said coldly. "Hate me if you must, for not being the man you wish I could be. But don't punish our child for it."

Honora sucked in her breath. Was that what she'd been doing? Punishing him? She hated the thought.

She bit her lip. "If you really want to be part of her life—"

"Her?" Nico's eyes lit up. "We're having a girl?"

She nodded. It might have made her happy, seeing the delight on his face, if it hadn't made her so sad. "Due in mid-September."

"A daughter," he whispered. "A child of my own."

"You don't have any other children? You're sure?"

He shook his head. "I've always been careful. I've always made utterly certain... I must have been careless that night." He gave a crooked smile. "Obviously."

Careless. That was one way of putting it. The lump in her throat became a razor blade. "Me too," she said in a low voice. "I blamed you...but I made my own choices. I could have insisted you use a condom. I could have chosen not to sleep with you at all." She lifted her gaze. "I took the risk. My choice. And I'll have to live with that for the rest of my life. But I won't let our baby pay the price."

"Does that mean you'll marry me?"

Honora held desperately to the last shreds of her dignity, and her hope for a family created out of love, not cold obligation. She shook her head. "But if you can really be a good father, then I'll let you share custody."

"Let me?" The satisfaction in his handsome face faded to anger. *"If* I can be a good father?"

She felt his coldness and raised her chin. "If you can cut back on the Scotch and come back to the world of the living. If you can actually be good to her."

"I already gave your grandfather my word I'd marry you."

She shrugged. "You should have asked me first. I have something else in mind."

"My chauffeur?"

Was he jealous? No, surely not. Nico Ferraro dated women by the score and tired of them quickly. If even a world-famous beauty like Lana Lee couldn't keep him, what chance did an ordinary girl like Honora have? She knew, to her core, that if she married him, he'd only break her heart.

"If you truly want to be a father, I will do everything I can to support that." She turned toward the beachfront mansion's windows. The storm had abated, and she could see silvery moonlight frosting the clouds scattered across the ocean's horizon. She said in a small voice, "But I can't marry you. I want to be loved."

Nico stared at her for a long moment.

"Maybe you're right," he said suddenly.

She blinked. "What?"

"It's clear nothing I say tonight will convince you."

Honora had been about to list more reasons why she could never, ever marry him. She felt strangely off-kilter by his sudden surrender. She told herself she was relieved. Wasn't she? "Oh. Good. How will we explain it to Granddad?"

"I'll talk to him. I owe him that much."

"Right now?"

"It's almost midnight." Nico went to the wet bar. For a moment, she thought he was going to pour more Scotch into his half-empty glass. Instead, he dumped it all down the sink and turned to her with a charming smile. "I'll take you back home in the morning. Until then, I bid you good night."

"Good night," she said faintly, her lips slightly parted as he turned and left the room without a word.

As she followed him up the sweeping staircase of the beach house, she could hardly believe it. She'd won. She'd actually won. Nico Ferraro had given up his desire to marry her.

So why didn't she feel more joyful about it?

CHAPTER FOUR

WAKING UP THE NEXT morning in the master bedroom of the Hamptons beach house, Nico smiled to himself, amazed at how well he'd slept. Getting out of bed, he stretched in his silk boxers, then went out on his balcony to breathe the fresh ocean air.

The summer storm had cleared out, leaving only beauty behind. Wispy clouds of pink and magenta and peach traced the eastern horizon in the vivid colors of dawn. The deep blue sky, growing lighter by the second, stretched as wide as the Atlantic. He felt like his future, too, was wide open. Nothing but blue skies and blue ocean, ripe with possibility.

First on his agenda: making Honora his wife.

He felt a zing of nervous energy at the thought, and decided to go for a run on the beach. He had to dig in the closet for exercise clothes because he hadn't brought any in his suitcase from Rome. The realization shocked him.

Before Christmas, he'd been very disciplined about intense daily exercise, as he was about everything. But since then, his only real exercise had been sparring in a boxing gym in Rome—and even that he'd only done out of self-preservation after an altercation with a random lawyer who'd tried to get his clients out of a real estate deal. Nico didn't remember much about the work he'd sunk himself into over the last six months, but he did remember the moment he'd lunged across the boardroom table and punched the man in the face.

He'd paid for it, of course. He'd settled out of court for a million euros. Pretty expensive way to let off steam. After that, he'd started expending his dark energy at the gym. Better to vent his anger wearing gloves and face guards fighting willing participants or, better yet, a gym bag. Other than that, he'd just worked all day, every day, until he collapsed with exhaustion on the sofa in his private office.

Last night was the first time in months that Nico had slept the whole night through. He marveled at how much better he felt. He hadn't known it was even possible for him to sleep ten hours.

He'd only had one drink last night—he'd thrown the rest down the sink. He'd wanted to prove a point to Honora, but he knew that wasn't the only reason he felt better.

He had a mission again. A totally impossible mission, just like when, as a penniless teenager, he'd vowed to be rich.

He would convince Honora Callahan to marry him.

True, he couldn't give her the romantic love she dreamed of. But he could offer so much more, more than enough to compensate. His fortune, of course. His name. Clearly, the marks of status that would appeal to most women didn't hold much weight with her. So he'd offer more.

He'd lure her with passion, and a partnership based on mutual respect, even friendship. He had to convince her that she could trust him to cherish and provide for them always. That was the most important thing. She had to know their daughter would be raised in a stable home and would always know she was adored, wanted and welcomed by both parents.

Compared to all that, what was some paltry thing like romantic love? Nothing but sickly sweet love poems and wilting roses.

As soon as he could prove to Honora that he'd never break his commitment to them, he knew she'd fall into his arms.

Thinking of it, Nico smiled to himself and ran a little faster on the edges of the white sandy beach, running on the packed wet section close to the blue-gray surf. The sea air felt fresh and new in the dawn. And that was how he felt. Fresh and new.

He'd changed tactics last night when he'd realized his heavy-handed marriage demand wasn't working. The more he'd insisted he wanted to marry her and that he intended to be a good husband and father, the more she'd argued with him. So he'd backed off. Insinuated he'd changed his mind about marriage.

He hadn't.

But he'd learned that in business, the most desirable acquisitions usually took extra time and care. It was her own free choice. She had to *want* to marry him.

So he would convince her.

Nico picked up the pace to a flat-out run, wet sand flying behind him on the beach in the early-morning light.

All he had to do was become the man she needed. A man who was ready to be a good husband, a good father.

He'd already stopped drinking. Next he would cut back on his working hours and return to a healthier life-style of exercise and sleeping in a proper bed. It was horrifying to Nico now, in the cold light of dawn, to realize how lost he'd been the last six months. Yes, he'd added millions to his company's bottom line by working with such monomaniacal focus. But he'd done that only out of desperate need for distraction. Other than the fistfight with the lawyer, he hardly remembered any of it. Because none of it mattered.

What difference did it make if Nico's net worth went up another hundred million? His father was dead. He'd never have the satisfaction of seeing the old man weep his regret that he'd rejected Nico as a boy, believing him unworthy of being his son.

He'd never been Nico's family. Honora, their daughter, their other children yet to come—they would be.

He just had to convince Honora he was worthy of her. And since their baby was due in around two and a half months, he was on the clock.

Checking his smartwatch, Nico saw he'd run five miles. He looked at his speed. Not bad, considering that yesterday he'd been a numb, pathetic workaholic without a reason to live. Now he was getting back to life, to his old discipline, he'd soon improve. With his new focus, he'd springboard to even greater wealth, greater power. Only now, instead of rubbing it in the face of that aristocratic bastard, Nico would bask in the glow of a loving wife and adoring children. He would be happy, damn it.

And hopefully *that* would leave his dead father spinning in his grave.

Turning around, he started running back toward his house five miles down the shore. He wouldn't put the mansion up for sale after all, he decided. They'd make memories here. Fill those bedrooms with children.

Just thinking of Honora, he felt his blood grow hot. He could hardly wait to have her in his bed. And this time, he'd make sure he remembered every delicious moment of touching her. He could hardly wait.

Maybe tonight. Or tomorrow. How long did it usually take for a man to prove himself worthy of a woman?

Whatever the usual time was, Nico would do it faster. And better.

Honora Callahan didn't stand a chance.

Was it hot in here, or was it just her?

"Thank you for the ride," Honora said, resisting the urge to fan herself. She felt a bead of sweat forming between her breasts. Because she was pregnant, she told herself fiercely. Not because she wanted him.

"My pleasure." Nico's voice was a low purr beside her. His hands were casual on the wheel as he wove the Lamborghini through highway traffic with confidence and grace. His dark eyes gleamed as he gave her a sensual smile. She gritted her teeth. Damn the man.

The morning after she'd refused his marriage proposal, it seemed cruel that he looked even more handsome and desirable than ever, in a white collared shirt that hugged his muscular torso and flat belly, the top two buttons undone around his thick neck, and wearing trim-fitting dark trousers over his powerful thighs.

He gave her a wicked grin. Realizing she was fanning herself, she stopped with a blush and clasped her hands firmly in her lap.

"It's July," she said sharply. "Aren't you hot?"

He shrugged. "I'm used to it."

His Italian leather shoe pressed on the gas. He looked relaxed, as if he'd had an amazing night's sleep and plenty of fresh air and exercise.

While Honora had just had the worst night she could remember. She'd felt anxious and tense in the beautiful guest room, staring up at the ceiling, questioning the choice she'd just made. Had she been utterly selfish, holding out for love instead of marrying the father of her baby?

Nico had offered her everything. Except his heart.

And after a lifetime of trying to make herself sweet and helpful and small, to take up as little space as possible, to feel less like a burden to the people she loved, she didn't think she could bear to live like that for the rest of her life. Was it selfish to want to be loved?

Honora finally fell asleep a few hours before dawn. When she'd woken up, it was midmorning, and the slant of warm golden light flooded the wide windows overlooking the Atlantic. Anxiety rushed through her as she glanced at the clock over the fireplace. She was going to be late!

Peeking into the hallway, she'd found her white sundress, folded with her white cotton bra and panties, clean and pressed as promised. She couldn't stand tight clothes anymore. This dress was stretchy, and with its spaghetti straps helped her stay cool in the summer heat. After getting dressed and putting on her sandals, she paused just long enough to brush her teeth and run a comb through her hair before she hurried downstairs.

She found Nico in the breakfast room, his dark hair still wet from the shower, drinking black coffee as he perused the morning's news. When she rushed in like a madwoman with her hair on fire, he looked up in surprise.

"Good morning." His voice was husky, his dark eyes glowing. "I trust you slept well."

Honora could hardly admit otherwise without revealing the emotional tumult inside her. "Yes. Thank you." She cleared her throat. "But I overslept. I need to leave now, if I'm going to get the train on time."

"The train?" Folding his paper, he looked bemused. "I told you I'd take you back to the city. You have an appointment?"

"At my doctor's. In three hours."

"Then we have plenty of time. Sit down." His dark eyes caressed her, making her feel shivery inside. "What would you like for breakfast?"

You, she thought, then kicked herself for even thinking such a traitorous thing. "Um…buttered toast?"

"We can do better than that."

Sitting at the farthest edge of the long table, she was soon tucking into a big plate of fruit, eggs and buttered toast, served by Sebastian the butler, who seemed to have warmed to her. Nico smiled when, blushing a little, she asked for tea with milk.

"So you like it," he said.

"I never thought of putting milk in herbal tea."

His smile widened to a wicked grin. "So I showed you something new."

Honora had bitten her lip as she remembered how he'd shown her all kinds of new things on Christmas night, things that made her shiver whenever she allowed them in her memory, kisses and touches and nibbles that would forever be imprinted on her skin.

Sitting beside him in the Lamborghini as they sped toward the city, Honora caught her breath. She had to get ahold of herself!

As they crossed the Queensboro Bridge, she looked out at the Manhattan skyline. Skyscrapers reached into the blue sky in a city that hummed like the buzzing center of the world. Or was it just the rush of blood through her own heart?

They arrived at her obstetrician's office on the West Side in record time.

"You can drop me off at the curb," she said quickly.

"I'd like to come."

Honora looked at him in surprise. "You want to go to my doctor's appointment?"

"I want to hear our daughter's heartbeat. I don't want to miss a thing."

"Okay. If you really want," she said, but as Nico looked for a place to park, she could barely contain her shock. Never, in all the years she'd known him as her grandfather's boss, had she ever seen Nico Ferraro give away his time to anyone.

He gave people money, of course. He paid his employees well and donated large sums to charities, gifts that were always splashed in the news as PR for Ferraro Developments Inc. And Nico had occasionally given her grandfather praise, or gifts arranged by one of his personal assistants. But spend an hour of his precious time on something that was not for his own direct benefit? Never.

And yet Nico was patient and attentive during the doctor's appointment, asking lots of questions. He squeezed Honora's hand during the ultrasound, and when he saw the outline of their baby on the screen, the small head, fingers and toes, Nico's handsome face filled with emotion.

"That's our baby," he whispered, and he lowered his head to kiss her.

It was barely a peck, just a friendly kiss. But still. It reminded her of the kiss he'd given her last night, a kiss that had made her want to forget every warning of self-preservation and fall into his arms.

But Honora had learned her lesson. No matter how interested and patient he seemed now, she knew his attention would wane. He wasn't the kind of man who would ever settle down—especially not with someone as average as Honora.

As they left the doctor's office, Nico held her hand, and in his other he clutched the ultrasound image of their baby. He kept smiling down at it. And it made hope rise unbidden inside her.

Did he really want to be a father? Did he mean it? Would it last?

Honora's phone rang.

"Are you back in the city?" Her grandfather's voice sounded odd.

"Yes, we're coming from my checkup."

"*We*? Your fiancé is with you?"

"Granddad, he's not—"

"When is he bringing you home?"

"Now." The sooner the better. Being with Nico was starting to make her want things she shouldn't.

"Good. Your doc's in midtown, right?"

"Near Lincoln Center—"

"See you soon." And her grandfather hung up. She stared at the phone with a frown, wondering why he was acting so weird. He'd acted weird last night, too. Not the bit with the rifle but afterward, when he'd pretended to be old and tired so he could return to the city immediately.

Had it just been an excuse to leave Honora and Nico alone, so they'd pick a wedding date? Or was it something else?

As she walked down the sidewalk in the bright July sunshine, a wave of foreboding went through her.

Nico said suddenly, "What do fathers usually drive? Minivans?"

"What?" She looked up, confused.

Seeing her face, Nico gave a low laugh. "I must sound like an idiot," he said ruefully as he opened the passenger door of the Lamborghini. She climbed in, carefully lowering herself into the low-slung seat. "I just don't know much about them."

"Babies?"

"Fathers."

Had he spent no time with his father at all growing up? "You don't need to rush out and buy a minivan. You already have tons of cars," she told him when he got in the driver's seat. "Just choose one with a back seat. An SUV is fine, or even a sedan like the Bentley."

She regretted mentioning the Bentley almost immediately. As he started the engine, he shot her a questioning glance.

"Rossini's in love with you, you know."

Honora looked out the window as they drove down the street. "Are you sure you don't mind driving all the way to Queens? I could take the subway."

"Of course I don't mind, and don't change the subject."

She gave a regretful sigh. "I know he is," she said in a small voice. "But I'm not sure what to do about it." She tilted her head. "What do *you* do? You must have lots of women fall in love with you."

Nico snorted. "No."

"How is that possible?"

He gave a shrug. "If any woman starts acting like she's in love with me, I'm extremely rude until she changes her mind."

She gave a low laugh, then grew thoughtful. "What about Lana Lee? She must have loved you to want to marry you."

Staring at the road, he said quietly, "I doubt it. She liked the press attention and lifestyle I could provide."

"Wasn't she already rich, as a movie star?"

"There's rich, and then there's *rich*," he pointed out. "But you're right. She didn't need me. She was just surprised when I broke up with her. She isn't used to it."

"Why did you propose to her in the first place if you didn't love her? I mean, *she* wasn't pregnant, was she?"

Nico shot her a sharp glance, and she felt her cheeks go hot. "Of course not. I told you. You're the first and only." His hands tightened on his steering wheel. "The reason I proposed to Lana is no longer relevant."

Honora waited, but he didn't explain his clear nonanswer. She tried to think of a way to ask probing questions without it being obvious. She couldn't.

"Was it because she was so famous and beautiful?" she said finally.

"You could say it was a mark of success. At least to a certain type of person."

As marrying Honora wouldn't be. The thought made her feel small.

"But still—" she tried to keep her voice casual "—you've dated lots of other women since we were together."

His forehead creased as he glanced at her in surprise. "Why do you think that?"

"Because you're so handsome and…" She caught herself, biting her lip hard. She couldn't seem to stop making a fool of herself. "Are you saying you haven't?"

Nico gave a low laugh. "I told you how I spent my time in Rome. Dating was the furthest thing from my mind. All I did was work." Changing gears, he looked at her. "Until you told me you were pregnant, and changed my life."

As they came out of the Midtown Tunnel into Queens, she gave him her grandfather's address. Heads turned as the Lamborghini passed by. Millionaires didn't live here in their sterile high-rises, like in Manhattan. Instead, this neighborhood was filled with small businesses and interesting neighbors, with streets rich with color and life. Before her parents had died, she'd lived in a small apartment around the block.

When he found a place to park along the street, four children, playing nearby on their scooters, came closer with big eyes.

"Keep an eye on my car, will you?" As Nico got out of the vehicle, he gave the little girl in front a friendly smile. "I'll pay you twenty dollars."

"Each?" demanded the lead kid, folding her arms. Nico gave a single nod, one CEO to another.

"You got it."

"Oh, hey, Honora," the girl said as Nico helped her out of the passenger seat.

"Hey, Luna."

"This guy your friend?"

Honora glanced at Nico. *Friend* seemed much nicer than *baby daddy.* "Yes, my friend."

"Hang on." The little girl huddled up with her friends, and then announced to Nico grandly, "We'll watch your car for free."

"Thanks," he said, amused. As the two of them

walked down the sidewalk, he looked at Honora. "They think highly of you."

She gave a shrug. "I help them with homework. Buy them Popsicles when it's hot. Last month, I helped Luna find her lost cat." She smiled at the memory. "We looked for hours, then found her hiding in a tree across the street."

Nico looked at her gravely. "Your friendship is a good thing to have."

She felt her cheeks go hot. "It's no big deal. Anyone would have done it." She cleared her throat. "The apartment's just up here."

Her grandfather's two-bedroom apartment was above a pizza shop on the avenue. She punched in the code, and once inside, they went up the stairs.

As she reached into her purse to get out the key, the apartment door suddenly opened in front of her. Her gray-bearded grandfather stood inside the doorway. He was still in his morning robe, though it was late afternoon.

And he wasn't alone.

"Mrs. Kowalczyk?" Honora gasped at sight of the sweet widowed lady who owned the flower shop where Honora worked part-time. "What are you doing here? Er…?"

Even to her innocent mind, it was obvious what Phyllis Kowalczyk had been doing. The plump, white-haired woman looked flushed and disheveled, as if she'd dressed in a hurry, with the buttons of her yellow blouse done up in the wrong places. The older couple stared back at them in shock, their cheeks red.

"How did you get here so fast?" her grandfather demanded indignantly. "You must have broken the speed limit!"

"Patrick," Phyllis said quietly, "you might as well tell them."

Her grandfather sighed. "Fine." Waving them inside, he led them into the tiny living room, with a window directly over the pizza shop's neon sign. "You should sit down."

Staring at her grandfather, Honora thought she had better. She fell heavily into the small, slightly saggy sofa. Nico sat beside her, neither of them touching.

Across from them, Patrick sat in his old chair and Phyllis in the chair beside him. They glanced at each other, smiling tenderly.

Holding her breath, Honora looked between them. "Are the two of you…?"

Patrick Burke looked proud and shy all at once, puffing out his chest like a teenager. "I've asked Phyllis to marry me."

Honora blinked, feeling dizzy. "I didn't even know you were dating."

"We weren't," Phyllis said. "We met sometimes in the shop, and around the neighborhood over the years. I fell hard." She looked at him. "But he wasn't free to be in a relationship. Not when you needed him."

Honora turned to her grandfather, flabbergasted. "I did?"

Patrick looked embarrassed. "My duty was to you, Honora. You'd already been through so much. I couldn't bring someone else into our apartment, into our lives. I couldn't be in a relationship. Especially when you were pregnant and alone." His wrinkled face lit up. "But when Nico agreed to take responsibility last night, and with the two of you starting a family of your own…" His eyes looked dreamy as he turned to Phyllis. "Now I'm free."

Honora felt an ache in her throat. It was just as she'd thought. She'd been a burden, keeping her grandfather from living the life he wanted. "I never meant to…"

"First thing I did when I got back here last night was tell Phyllis I loved her." Patrick looked at Phyllis. "I'd wanted to say it for so long."

"I know," Phyllis said, reaching out for his hand. "I know."

Honora stared at the grandfather who'd raised her. She barely recognized him in this moment.

"You love her?" she whispered. Granddad had never said those words to her, not once, not even when she was a child. She felt suddenly more alone than she ever had. Taking a deep breath, she pasted a happy smile on her face. "So you're moving in together?"

"Moving in?" Patrick looked shocked. "Like a couple of hippies? My intentions are honorable!" he protested, then gave Phyllis a sly glance. "Though last night, one thing led to another. This afternoon, too…"

"Patrick!" Phyllis was blushing. "Stop!"

"Anyways…" He cleared his throat with a *harrumph*. "We got the license this morning. We're getting married tomorrow."

"Tomorrow?"

"Don't worry, dear," Phyllis said kindly. "We won't steal your thunder. We're going down to city hall. No big ceremony or fuss. Just a couple of witnesses, then we'll leave on our honeymoon."

"Which is more to the point." Patrick grinned. She gave him a mock glare.

"I'd signed up for a horticulture cruise," Phyllis rushed to explain. "Two weeks down the coast, and it leaves tomorrow night. We're going to take it together, as a honeymoon."

"It all seems so fast." Honora's voice was a little hoarse.

"Not fast enough." Her grandfather looked at Phyllis. "We'd be married already if it weren't for the twenty-four-hour waiting period."

The older woman turned to Honora. "But listen to us going on and on about ourselves. I haven't congratulated you on your engagement, dear." She smiled broadly. "Such happy news. And don't worry—" she held up her hand "—I've already replaced you at the store."

"I told her I'll work for free," Patrick chortled.

Honora stared at him in shock. "You're leaving the rooftop garden? But it's your passion!"

He shook his head. "Honestly, the way my arthritis has been acting up in winter, I was ready to try something new. Besides, *Phyllis* is my passion now, and she says life begins at seventy."

"It does," she agreed. He looked at her.

"Letting myself love you has already changed me," he said quietly. "It's let the light in."

He suddenly seemed younger than Honora, in spite of all his gray hair. And she saw it all clearly.

For thirteen years, he'd given up his own dreams to

take care of his grandchild. Even after Honora had become an adult, he'd still had to put her first. After being widowed for decades, he'd pushed away the woman he loved. He'd obviously thought he had no choice, since Honora had only had a part-time job, no apartment of her own, and then to top it off, she'd accidentally gotten pregnant.

She'd known she was a burden. She just hadn't realized how much of one. She felt sick with shame.

"I guess I'll need a new gardener," Nico said dryly.

"Yup."

"Probably for the best," he responded. "Though I'll never find another gardener who can coax daffodils so well."

Patrick grinned. "No, that you won't."

"Darling," Phyllis said, "I need to go check on the shop—"

"Right." He abruptly stood up. "And I'm sure you two have places to be." Tilting his head, Patrick said to Honora, "So did you set a date?"

Rising in his turn, Nico cleared his throat. "Actually, I should tell you, we—"

Grabbing his hand, Honora squeezed it. "We'll wait to get married until you return from your honeymoon."

She stared hard at Nico, willing him to play along.

"Yes," he said. "In two weeks."

"Perfect." The older couple beamed at them.

"I'll say goodbye, then," Nico said to Honora, and started to leave. But as he did, Phyllis elbowed her grandfather in the ribs.

"Right. The thing is," Patrick said, "Phyllis is having

her apartment painted, so she'll be staying here tonight. Even though it's not strictly proper." His cheeks were pink as he cleared his throat. "You're very welcome to stay too, of course, Honora. At least until you move in with Nico after your marriage."

It was like being a deer and seeing the approaching headlights of the car that was about to hit you. She stared at her grandfather, frozen.

He smiled. "But I thought…why make you pretend? I'm sure you'd rather stay at the penthouse immediately. I can't fool myself that you're not sleeping together, not when…" His eyes fell briefly on Honora's belly. "So if you'd rather…"

"But of course, you'll always be welcome here, dear," Phyllis added. "It's your home."

"Thanks." This place *had* been Honora's home, but it suddenly wasn't anymore. The thought of staying here, butting in on their love affair, being a burden, feeling like an outsider…

"You're right, Granddad." She forced herself to smile. "The truth is, if you don't mind, I'd rather stay with Nico tonight."

The other couple looked relieved.

"I figured. And I can hardly criticize you for impropriety, can I?" her grandfather said with a sheepish grin. Then he blinked, reaching to squeeze her hand. "I'm so happy for both of us, Honora." His eyes wandered to his fiancée. "Have you ever felt this way before?"

Honora looked up at Nico, who was watching her with dark, inscrutable eyes.

"Never," she whispered.

CHAPTER FIVE

"THANKS FOR NOT blowing my cover," Honora said as he packed her small overnight bag into the Lamborghini, then helped her into the car. "I'll tell them the truth after they're back from the honeymoon."

"I'm glad to have you stay with me tonight," Nico said honestly. It had been a lucky break, he thought. And with a little more luck, by the time Patrick and Phyllis returned from their honeymoon, the fake engagement would be a real one.

"Do you mind dropping me off at a hotel?" she asked as he got into the driver's seat.

He looked at her. "Hotel?"

"Just for one night, until they're safely married and away." Her green eyes looked sad. "Otherwise he might cancel his wedding if he thinks he's still stuck with me."

He frowned. What a strange way to put it. "*Stuck* with you?"

She looked out the window at the dark city, lights sparkling hollowly against the glass. "I'll figure something out by the time they're back. Find a new place to live."

"Or come live with me."

"And I'll need a new job," she said, as if she hadn't heard. She gave him a crooked smile. "You need a new gardener for your rooftop terrace."

He snorted. "You're the mother of my child. I'm not hiring you as a gardener."

Honora looked at him, then sighed. "I guess you're right. It would be awkward. But I need to do something. Two weeks isn't very long."

"I'll always provide for you, Honora. You and the baby both."

Her green eyes looked sad. "Thank you, but the last thing I want to be is a burden."

Was she serious? "You're not—"

"And I know you promised Granddad you'd come tomorrow and be a witness at their wedding, but you don't have to. I can ask Benny instead."

Nico's hands tightened on the steering wheel. "Rossini?"

"He's a friend," she said, a little defensively.

Friend or not, Nico made a mental note to tell his residential staffing manager, Sergio, to reassign the young chauffeur to a different job on the other side of the world. He didn't care what or where, as long as he wasn't around Honora.

Nico protected what was his. And she was his.

He just needed more time to convince her of that.

"Are you hungry?" he suggested suddenly.

She grinned. "I'm pregnant. I'm *always* hungry."

"How about Au Poivre?"

She looked at him incredulously. "That fancy place downtown?"

"They make a good steak."

Honora snorted. "Sure, if you don't mind paying two hundred bucks for it. And don't you have to book a table six months in advance?"

"What sounds good to you, if not steak?"

She pondered. "Chicken potpie?"

"The owner's a friend of mine." He pulled out his phone. "I'll tell him we're on the way."

Thirty minutes later, as a valet whisked away the Lamborghini, Nico escorted her into the restaurant, which was decorated in an old French country style, with worn brick walls and heavy timber braces across the ceiling. The owner himself escorted them to a prime table beside the tall, rustic French fireplace, which, since it was July, was filled with a cluster of lit candles instead of a roaring fire.

"I am glad to see you again, Mr. Ferraro," the man said warmly. "I'll never forget how you moved heaven and earth to settle our real estate dispute."

Nico felt embarrassed. "I pointed you in the right direction, that's all. The right lawyer…"

"Not only that, you paid for it. We never would have survived lockdown if not for your investment."

Honora was looking between them with big eyes. Nico was ready for this conversation to be over. He cleared his throat. "You make the best steak in New York."

"Thank you." The owner beamed at him, then turned

to Honora. "My chef is already preparing your chicken potpie, *madame*."

"You're too kind." Now she was the one to look embarrassed. "I'm sorry to be so much trouble."

"No trouble, no trouble at all, *madame*. For a friend of Mr. Ferraro, our menu has no end. But I fear it will take a bit of time to prepare. I am so sorry. I'll bring an appetizer while you wait." He bowed, then turned to Nico. "Your usual Scotch?"

"I'll have sparkling water tonight."

"Of course. And the lady?"

"The same," she said, surprised. The man departed with another bow. She looked at Nico. "Are you trying to impress me? If you are, it's working."

He shrugged. "I did the restaurant a very small service, and invested a little money. It was nothing…"

"I mean that you've stopped drinking." Their eyes met across the small candlelit table.

"You suggested I stop," he said gruffly. "I was smart enough to take that advice."

"Why would you care what I think?"

His voice was quiet. "Your opinion matters a great deal."

Honora's eyes were wide as waiters brought sparkling water to the table, along with an *amuse-bouche* of fig, walnut and goat cheese wrapped with prosciutto.

As Nico sipped the water, Honora reached for one of the appetizers, then froze. Leaning forward across the table, she whispered, "People are staring at us."

Looking around, he saw well-heeled patrons at the other tables watching them, some surreptitiously, others openly. Turning back to Honora, he shrugged. "It happens. Don't worry about it."

She looked down at her white sundress and sandals in dismay. "Is it because I'm not dressed up?"

"People are always interested in the women I date," he said matter-of-factly.

Her blush deepened as her lips parted. "But you and I...we're not dating!"

"They don't know that." Looking at her in the candlelight, he added quietly, "And neither do I."

Biting her lip, she looked up at him with big eyes, her lovely face stricken. She leaned back in her chair. Her hand seemed to tremble as she reached for her water glass and took a long drink.

"This place is beautiful inside," she said finally. "It feels almost medieval."

"Not quite. That wall over there—" he nodded towards an exposed brick wall "—dates back to when the city was New Amsterdam. I celebrated making my first million here, after I moved to New York. The architecture reminded me of Europe. I liked it."

"Because you were born there?" At his surprised look, she smiled. "The housekeeper told me. I *have* been in your life for over ten years, even if you didn't notice."

Nico wondered now how it was possible that he'd never noticed his gardener's granddaughter. Looking at Honora now, here, in the body-skimming sundress with thin straps that revealed her full pregnant glory, she looked intoxicatingly beautiful, her dark hair tumbling over bare shoulders. Her big eyes shone in the candlelight.

"I lived in Rome till I was eight," he said. "Then my mother married an American and moved us to Chicago."

"Does your family still live there?"

He blinked at the word *family*. Was that what they'd been? "My mother died when I was seventeen. My stepfather last year."

"I'm sorry." Honora put her hand over his on the wooden table. Her hand was soft, comforting, warm. "Were you close?"

Close. His throat closed. He still couldn't bear to remember his mother's death, the silent cancer that had showed no symptoms until it was too late. There had been an experimental treatment that might have saved her, if they'd had three hundred thousand dollars to pay for it. Desperate, Nico had buried his pride and phoned Prince Arnaldo. It was the first and only time he'd ever spoken directly to his father. "Please," he'd choked out in Italian, "help her. And I'll never ask you for anything again."

"Why would I give you so much money?" the man had replied coldly. "I'm not some fool to throw away my fortune on quack treatments with no chance of success."

"But you owe her. You owe us."

"Maria is nothing to me, and neither are you." And he'd hung up.

Arnaldo had been right about one thing—the experimental treatment had turned out to be a mirage. But it might have saved her, Nico told himself stubbornly. His mother might have been the exception. After her death, Nico had taken his hurt and rage and thrown himself into working around the clock. Starting at eighteen, he'd bought his first Chicago property with credit, using his beat-up Mustang as collateral. He'd gotten lucky when a car wash chain had offered to buy the land from him at nearly double the price. He'd taken that profit and moved to New York, determined to make himself so rich and powerful that he could never be hurt again.

But after he'd become rich, he'd found he still felt an overwhelming restlessness inside.

That was when he'd decided to make Prince Arnaldo Caracciola pay—for everything.

"No," Nico said in a low voice. "We weren't close. But she was still my mother."

Honora didn't move her hand from his. "I'm sorry," she said quietly. "Like I said. I know how it feels."

She couldn't possibly know how he felt. But as she pulled her hand away, he thought how pretty she was, how enticing, with her pink lips and warm green eyes, as alive as a sunlit forest.

Nico changed the conversation to lighter things, to a project he was building in London that he knew would interest her, because it was surrounded by five acres of green space. It seemed like mere minutes before their dinners were served, chicken potpie for her, and his usual steak in peppercorn sauce. As they ate, he enjoyed listening to her talk, her brightness, her cheerful optimism, her kindness—all so different from the entitled world-weariness and humblebragging he was accustomed to hearing from mistresses. Honora Callahan was honest and enthusiastic and lovely. She was a breath of fresh air. Any man would be lucky to have her in his life, he thought suddenly.

"This potpie was amazing." Setting her fork down on her empty plate, she sighed in pleasure. Her full breasts and baby bump pressed against the small table as she leaned forward. "By the way, thanks for being with me at Granddad's today. I'm not sure I would have survived otherwise…"

He forced himself to lift his gaze from her curves. "I'm glad I could help."

Honora shook her head wryly. "He actually said he loved her. *Aloud.* I can hardly believe it." She gave a wistful smile. "He's never said that to me, not once."

Her tone was cheerful, but he could feel an ocean of sadness beneath it. He recognized that ocean. Everything he'd done as a man had been in order to leave that sad, lonely boy behind and become powerful, and impervious to hurt. He shrugged.

"My mother used to say it to me all the time." He took a drink of the sparkling water. "She never meant it."

"I'm sure she loved you." But her voice was uncertain.

He gave a small smile. "It's hard to love the person who blows up your life and forces you to give up your dreams and live in poverty."

"Your father didn't help?"

He shook his head. "He was a married aristocrat. She was a maid in his palace. The last thing he was going to do was recognize me as his own."

The words hung in the air like a toxic cloud. He'd never said them to anyone before.

"Oh, Nico, how could he?" she said softly. "He didn't even pay child support?"

He realized his hand was clenching the edge of the oak table so tightly that it hurt. Strange. One might think he was still angry about it. But he felt nothing. "My mother tried, but she was young, without family, and no one to give her advice. And he was powerful, un-touchable, behind guarded palace walls." He took a deep breath. "She worked three jobs to support us. Then she met my stepfather, who worked in the American base. He told her loved her and swore he'd take care of her."

"What happened?"

"She married him and we moved to the States. She thought her life would be easier, but it wasn't. She never felt at home in Chicago. Then Joe started complaining that she wasn't the same girl he'd fallen in love with." He gave a hard smile. "He complained about me, too."

"Why? What did you do?"

"I loved reminding him he wasn't my father, and had no right to tell me what to do. Even at age eight, I hated him. I felt like an outsider in my own home. Then he told my mother he'd fallen in love with someone else, and I hated him even more for making her cry. They didn't have any assets. After the divorce, we were even poorer than before."

Twilight was falling outside the lead glass windows, leaving a trail of violet across her bare shoulders. "I'm sorry…"

"He told her he loved her all the time, at the beginning. My father apparently said it to her, too, during their affair. They both told her they felt true love that would last forever."

Honora looked at him in the flickering candlelit restaurant. "No wonder you think so little of love."

Nico shrugged. "It's a momentary emotion at best. At worst, it's manipulation. A way to trick people into surrendering their lives."

"My grandfather used to say feelings didn't matter," she said in a small voice. "What was important was family, duty, being true to one's word."

"He's right." But she looked sad, so he changed the subject. "I'm getting some coffee. Would you like dessert? Chocolate cake with raspberries? Strawberry tart?"

She took a deep breath, then tried to smile. "The tart, please."

Turning away, he gave a small gesture to a waiter.

When they finally left the restaurant, Nico realized they were the last guests there, and had been talking for hours. To make amends to the waiters for keeping the table, he quietly left a five-thousand-dollar tip.

"Thank you for a lovely evening." Honora took his arm as they walked out into the moonlight. "And the food! I'm afraid it's spoiled me for all other chicken potpie. And strawberry tarts."

His glance lingered on her as the valet collected the Lamborghini. The summer night was warm as city lights sparkled in the skyscrapers looming above the slender lane.

"But now it's over." Honora looked wistful again. "Is there an affordable hotel nearby?"

"There's no reason to stay in a hotel."

"I told you I couldn't possibly go back home tonight, with Granddad and Phyllis there."

"Stay with me."

"With you?" She swallowed, then shook her head. "Thank you, but I couldn't possibly."

"No strings. You can stay in the guest room. I promise I won't touch you, Honora, for as long as you're staying with me. Not unless you ask." His gaze fell to her lips as he added huskily, "No matter how much I want to."

Staying with Nico would be a big mistake. Honora knew it before the valet even pulled the Lamborghini up in front of the restaurant.

"Guest room?" she repeated, then shook her head. "I couldn't impose."

"You keep using words like *burden* and *imposition*—words that make no sense to me. How much clearer can I be that I want you?"

She bit her lip. "But—"

His eyes gleamed. "It's just a night in my guest room, Honora. Not marriage vows."

She hesitated. What was she afraid of? That she'd fall into bed with him? No. Of course she wouldn't. She told herself she'd learned that lesson. And as he said, it was just crashing at his place for a night, not marriage vows. She exhaled. "All right. Thank you."

Nico gave her a small smile as he opened her car door, helping her inside.

They drove north to midtown. Pulling into his residential building's parking garage, he punched in his code, which lifted the gate into his exclusive parking area. He parked near his Mercedes G-Wagen, Tesla and the Bentley.

Lifting her overnight bag onto his shoulder, he helped her out of the low-slung car. He didn't drop her hand as they took the elevator to Nico's penthouse on the skyscraper's top two floors.

Nico's hand felt so good in her own. She shivered. He was so powerful, so broad-shouldered, towering over her. She wondered what the penthouse staff, who'd all watched Honora grow up, would think if they saw their billionaire boss holding her hand like this.

But by now they already knew about her pregnancy. Her grandfather hadn't exactly been discreet, and Benny knew too, as well as the staff at the Hamptons house. There'd likely be general gossip about Nico's pregnant date at Au Poivre, too. Soon, everyone would know she was Nico Ferraro's unwed baby mama.

She glanced at him out of the corner of her eye. He'd wanted to marry her, and she'd refused him. No one would ever believe *that*.

The elevator doors opened directly into the penthouse with its wide, sparsely decorated spaces and hard, modern furniture that seemed designed to impress, rather than be comfortable. But she'd always loved the big windows with the views of Manhattan, and the rooftop garden on the terrace was filled with flowers for nine months of the year.

Nico followed her gaze to the hard-edged furniture. "It doesn't look very baby-friendly, does it?"

"No," she agreed.

"You can help me figure out how to change it. And turn the guest room into a warm, cozy nursery." He grimaced. "Obviously my usual interior designer doesn't do warm and cozy."

"You want a nursery?"

"Sure. If we're sharing custody, sometimes the baby will be here. She'll need a place to stay."

Honora stared at him in dismay. Her mind hadn't gotten that far—imagining what would happen as they raised the baby separately. But of course Nico was right. Sometimes he and their daughter would have joys and make memories that Honora wouldn't share, because she wouldn't be with them.

And someday, when Nico got married, he'd have a family. And if Honora was very lucky, she would someday do the same. But their daughter would always go back and forth between them, never really at home anywhere.

"I wish this all could be different," she whispered.

Nico looked at her. "Why did you sleep with me at Christmas, Honora?" he said suddenly. "You weren't drunk."

She looked down at her sandals. "I told you." She spoke quietly. "I thought I was in love with you."

"And now?"

"Now…" She looked away. "I hate the thought of you raising our baby here without me. Each of us someday marrying someone else, starting a new family."

His voice was low. "You said that was what you wanted."

"None of this is what I wanted," she choked out, then turned away. Grabbing her overnight bag, she fled for the guest room before he could see the tears in her eyes. "I'm going to bed…"

Climbing into the big, empty bed of the penthouse guest room, Honora looked out the windows. Stretching up into the inky black sky, skyscrapers glittered like stars.

Why had she slept with Nico?

Why had she taken the subway to his penthouse on Christmas Day, telling her grandfather she urgently had to pick up a book she'd left there—for a homework assignment that wasn't even due till January? And why, when she'd found Nico brooding and alone, had she decided to stay?

Closing her eyes, she remembered that darkening afternoon, when she'd found him sitting alone on the hard furniture, staring at the flickering fire, beneath the wan lights of the Christmas tree. She'd hoped for a glimpse of him, that was all. Nico Ferraro was always surrounded by beautiful women, or friends as ruthless and powerful as himself.

She'd been shocked to find him alone. He'd looked at her, and the expression on his handsome face had starkly mirrored her own loneliness.

Her whole life, she'd felt like she had to earn her right to exist. By being cheerful. By being helpful. No one liked a girl who was selfish. Selfish girls caused parents to die in car crashes. If her grandfather hadn't taken her in, Honora would have gone to foster care. In the back of her mind, she'd always feared that if she were ever too much trouble, then perhaps he might send her away.

So seeing her same loneliness reflected in Nico's dark eyes, Honora had felt so drawn to him that she forgot to be afraid. She'd sat beside him on the sofa.

"I know how you feel," she'd whispered, as the fire-light flickered in the room.

"How can you?" His expression had been blank as he took another sip of the drink in his hand. She saw a half-empty bottle of Scotch on the end table. But his words weren't slurred. He seemed in perfect command of his senses, only sad.

With a deep breath, she'd said quietly, "For most of my life, I've felt alone, too."

Nico had turned to her. His dark eyes seemed to devour her whole, as if he were truly seeing her for the first time. And then, leaning forward, he'd suddenly taken her in his arms and kissed her.

Their passion had been a revelation. The happiest night of her life—cut short because she'd had to slip away at midnight, while Nico was still sleeping, to take the subway back home, so her old-fashioned grand-father wouldn't worry, or know what she'd been up to.

But the next morning, Honora had been tired but shyly happy as she accompanied Patrick to work at the penthouse. She'd wondered how Nico would greet her, if he'd take her in his arms and immediately make his claim. She dreamed about him telling her grandfather straight out that they were in love, about him asking for her grandfather's permission to court her. It had been a delicious fantasy.

But Nico hadn't been there. The housekeeper, Janet, had crisply informed them that their boss had already left for Rome, with no immediate plans to return.

Honora had felt like a fool. How could she have ever dared hope that she'd meant anything to him at all?

But yesterday, Nico had asked her to marry him. He wanted her. And she'd refused him. Her brain, her heart couldn't quite believe it.

She slept hard, in a dreamless sleep, and even when she woke, she felt like she was in a strange dream all day. She showered and put on sandals and a knit purple sundress with spaghetti straps. She went to the courthouse with Nico, who was wearing a white shirt and dark trousers. He drove the Bentley himself, since Benny Rossini had been suddenly and inexplicably transferred to another job.

She watched her grandfather, grinning and obviously beside himself with joy in his coat and tie, speaking marriage vows in front of a judge, before he kissed his new bride, who was wearing a simple white dress. Nico insisted on taking them all out for a late lunch, and then drove them to the docks to board their cruise ship.

Her grandfather seemed to shine with some brilliant inner light. Was that what love was? Should Honora hold out for the thing that everyone said made life worthwhile?

Or was it all just an illusion, as Nico had said? She thought of his mother and love that promised to last forever but swiftly died. Even her own parents, hadn't they both believed, at least when they were dating, that they were in love?

"Do you want me to take you home?" Nico asked quietly as he drove her away from the docks.

She thought of the small Queens apartment. Somehow it no longer felt like home. Even with it empty, she would feel like an interloper in a space that now belonged to the married couple.

"No," she said in a low voice. She looked at him. "Can I stay with you tonight?"

Nico's dark eyes widened but he didn't ask questions, only stepped on the gas.

When they arrived back at the penthouse, it was just past sunset. Honora went straight out to the terrace garden.

Outside, the rising moon traced lines of silver over the ivy climbing the walls of the garden, and lights dangled from every trellis, making it look like a fairyland.

She took a deep breath of the cooling air, breathing in the scent of honeysuckle, rose, gardenia. After so many hours spent here, this garden had always felt like home, even more than the tiny Queens walk-up apartment. It was her home. Her heart.

Which suddenly felt like it was breaking.

"Honora." Nico's voice was husky behind her. "What is it?"

She turned to face him, fighting back tears. "I don't want you to have your own nursery."

Nico came closer, towering over her, making her feel petite and feminine by comparison. He started to reach for her, then stopped himself, dropping his hands. "This pregnancy wasn't planned, by either of us," he said quietly. "But maybe it's fate. The start of something wonderful, for both of us. You know I want to be our baby's father, Honora. I want to be your husband." Looking down at her without touching, he whispered, "Whatever your dreams are, let me try to make them come true."

Honora's heart was pounding as she looked up at him.

Nico was so handsome, so broad-shouldered and powerful, standing in the rooftop garden in the moonlight. It seemed like a scene out of a movie, in which he'd start suddenly waltzing with her beneath the sea of lights sparkling in the velvety black sky with the glass and steel skyscrapers all around them.

Whatever your dreams are, let me try to make them come true.

But her greatest dream had always been to be loved.

"I don't want to feel like a burden. Never again…"

"A burden?" He looked incredulous. "Are you insane? Don't you understand how much I want you?"

"Because of the baby…"

"You're right. What do I know about children? I need you to teach me how to be the parent I want to be. But it's more than that. I *like* you, Honora. I respect you. I want you as my partner. My friend. I want you at my side." He whispered, "I want you in my bed."

She wanted all those things, too. But if it meant she'd never be loved, would the exchange be worth it?

Was it possible that Nico was right? That the dream Honora had hungered for all her life—love—was at best a passing emotion and at worst a manipulation?

Maybe there were more important things. Like kindness. Trust. Family. Loyalty. Friendship. *Passion.*

Her gaze fell to his lips, and she yearned for his touch. She knew he wanted her, too.

But she also knew he would keep his promise.

All around them on the terrace, skyscrapers stretched up into the night, their windows sparkling bigger and brighter than the stars.

She trusted him, Honora suddenly realized. She believed he would keep his word. That one simple fact changed everything.

He wouldn't touch her.

But there was nothing to stop *her* from touching him…

With an intake of breath, Honora threw her arms around him and lifted her lips passionately to his.

He froze in surprise, then as her mouth claimed his, he wrapped his powerful arms around her and kissed her back hungrily.

"Thank heaven," he whispered against her skin when they finally pulled apart. "Not being able to touch you was killing me."

"We can't have that." She looked up at him. "If you can commit to a lifetime," she said in a small voice, "if you're sure, I'll marry you, Nico."

His dark eyes lit up. "You won't regret it," he said huskily. "I'll make you happy. You and the child both. I swear it."

Honora prayed he was right and tried not to hear the desperate howl of her heart. She didn't need him to love her, she told herself. Just giving their baby a loving, secure home, being friends, being lovers, would be enough. It *would*.

And now, it would have to be.

CHAPTER SIX

WINNING WAS TORTURE.

Being kissed by Honora was paradise. Nico gloried in the feel of her petite, lush body in his arms. Her baby bump and full breasts pushed against his flat belly. Her lips were soft and warm, and as they parted for his, a small sigh came from the back of her throat.

Standing on the penthouse terrace in the cooling summer night, after she'd agreed to marry him, he'd felt the wind blow against his skin like the promise of a new life. For a moment he'd felt dizzy as he held her tight. He'd wanted that moment to last forever.

And he'd also wanted it to end immediately, by lifting her in his arms and carrying her inside, to his bed. But no. Honora wanted to wait for their wedding night. So the next two weeks—filled with agonizingly delicious kisses, but no sex—were agony for Nico.

"I want it to be special," she said quietly. "This time, I want it to feel real."

He then tried to persuade Honora to wed immediately, elope to Las Vegas on his private jet. But she'd held firm, wanting to wait and have a real wedding after her grandfather returned from his honeymoon.

"All right." Nico had sighed, giving in with all the grace he could muster. "I did promise to fulfill all your dreams. You should have the wedding you want."

She'd looked startled. "It's not for me. Weddings are for family and friends. For our baby. For the *community*."

Which was so opposite to Nico's usual way of thinking that he hadn't even known how to argue. To his own mind, all he wanted to do was marry her and start the honeymoon today. She was living in the guest room of his penthouse. So close! But so far away!

They kissed, of course. Constantly. He would grab her in the hallway, at breakfast, at dinner, and lean her against the wall, against the sofa, holding her tight and ravishing her with kisses until they both went weak in the embrace. He felt like an unsatisfied teenage virgin, voracious in his hunger and need.

Two weeks seemed like torture. He felt like he'd never waited for anything so long.

But apparently two weeks was lightning fast for wedding planning. When Honora had suggested that they simply order a cake, hire some friends of hers who were musicians and buy a bouquet ready-made from Phyllis's shop, he'd wanted to make the ceremony more special for her, so he'd convinced her to hire a wedding planner.

"That would leave me more time to decorate the nursery," she'd said, stroking her cheek thoughtfully. "Although it seems like a silly thing to hire out."

"I just want to make your life easier."

"Fine," she'd said with a sigh. He'd had the feeling she was indulging him, but he wanted to take care of her. When he'd found her pulling weeds in the rooftop garden, he'd quickly arranged for Sergio to hire new gardeners, a talented middle-aged couple who worked as a team. Honora had liked them immediately, but she couldn't resist pointing out smugly, "See? It took *two people* to replace Granddad!"

Even with a wedding planner, she was very busy, bustling around to help the man select flowers, food, colors. She and Nico spent one obligatory afternoon with his lawyers, signing the prenup that his phalanx of attorneys had insisted was necessary. Honora rolled her eyes at the mention of settlements, seeming not to care. But in this, as in everything, he made sure his terms were generous. The longer they were married, the more alimony she would receive if they ever divorced.

But Nico didn't like to even think of her leaving. He knew their marriage would last.

He loved seeing her joy as she decorated their baby's nursery in soft pink and cream, filling it with books and a crib, buying tiny little clothes that seemed doll-sized to his eyes. Nico, for his part, contributed a six-foot-tall white teddy bear selected by Giles, his assistant at the New York office. Gifts weren't Nico's thing. Anyway, at the moment he was so distracted by lust that he could barely even pretend to work, or care about the land his company was trying to procure in Dubai. It felt like their wedding day would never come.

Then, suddenly, it did.

They'd decided on a beachside wedding at his home

in the Hamptons. The weather dawned clear and bright, the previous day's mugginess swept away by the fresh Atlantic breeze.

Around them, tufts of long grass laced gently rolling sand dunes. The chairs faced a wedding arch laced with white and pink flowers, on the edge of the grassy bluff overlooking the blue ocean.

The guest list was small, only about a hundred people, as Honora had wanted only close friends and family. "Just people we truly love, who love us, people we want to support our marriage." Honora, of course, had many such people. Nico had struggled to come up with anyone who fit that description. So much of his life before now had been about climbing the ladder, about becoming rich and powerful, all to try to punish and impress someone who was now dead.

Did he really care about any of the people he called friends? Or was he just using them—as they used him?

But that had reminded him of one person he felt a little guilty about. He gave her name to the wedding planner, wondering if Lana Lee would even show, and half hoping she wouldn't, so he could tell himself he'd done what he could and forget about it.

Other than his ex-fiancée, he only managed to think of one true friend, who was more than a business rival or colleague. Theo Katrakis was a fellow self-made billionaire, an outsider like Nico—and a notorious womanizer who had similarly reached the age of thirty-six without a wife. But they'd watched a few football games together, done some race car driving on a lark, and once had actually had a personal conversation in which they'd discovered they'd both been educated in hard luck streets—Nico in Rome, Theo in Athens.

But now, Nico was wondering about the rightness of choosing him as his best man.

"No sight of the bride yet," Theo said in a low voice. The two men, dressed in sleek tuxedos, stood beneath the vivid pink roses in the wedding arch, watching as the guests arrived for the late-morning beachside ceremony. "You can still make a run for it."

Nico looked at his friend and was amazed to see he was serious. The Greek really thought Nico might desert Honora at the altar, in front of all her friends, after he'd given his promise to marry her. "You're my best man, Theo," he bit out. "You're supposed to be supportive."

"I *am* being supportive," he said cheerfully. "Run while you can."

Nico scowled. "You suck at being a best man."

"*You* suck at being a groom, since you wouldn't even let me throw you a bachelor party, which is really the whole point."

Nico was irritated. "Hey, anytime you want to leave…"

"Before I see if the maid of honor is worth seducing? Not on your life."

Baring his teeth in a smile for the benefit of the arriving guests, he said, "Maybe you just shouldn't talk."

"Nico," a woman's voice said behind him.

Whirling around, Nico saw Lana Lee coming across the grass from the house.

"Lana," he said in a low voice. He took a deep breath

as he looked at his former fiancée. "I didn't think you would come."

"Didn't you want me to?" She looked elegant as always, with her glossy black hair tied back in a long ponytail, wearing a chic dark dress that draped perfectly over her model-thin body. Her sunglasses were movie-star-big, and no wonder. She was one of the most famous actresses in the world, specializing in blockbuster action films. "I was close by, shooting a film in New York."

"It's good to see you."

"Let's cut the crap." She tilted her head. "Why did you invite me?"

Yes, why? "I thought that things ended…badly between us."

"So you thought inviting me to your quickie wedding to some new girlfriend would make it better?" She took off her sunglasses. Her lovely face was blank. "My therapist said I'd get closure by seeing you. That's the only reason I'm here."

"Closure?"

"You used me," she said. "You made me think you loved me, proposed marriage, then dumped me without any reason." She gave a humorless smile. "I'm curious to see if you'll do the same thing to your new fiancée. Is it true what I heard? You knocked up your maid?"

"Honora was never my maid." Nico set his jaw. He was starting to feel seriously annoyed. Why had he ever thought it was a good idea to invite his ex to his wedding? Maybe Theo was right when he'd said weddings were an unnecessary evil. He took a deep breath.

"I wanted to tell you I was sorry. I never meant to hurt you."

Lana stared at him then said, "You never thought of me at all. If I were a good person, I'd warn your bride about how selfish you are."

He set his jaw. "Oh, come on, Lana. Don't try to pretend we were some great love affair. I wasn't *using* you. We were using each other. You enjoyed the lifestyle, the extra attention right before awards season. Don't make it out to be something it wasn't. I only hurt your pride, not your heart."

She glared at him, clearly not listening. "How pregnant is she?"

"Seven months."

"Seven! You must have gotten her pregnant just days after you dumped me."

He forced himself to be honest. "Hours."

She looked at him with loathing. "Heaven help this girl if she ever loves you."

"She won't. She's too smart."

His ex-fiancée gave a low laugh. "That's the best news I've heard all day. In that case, I hope you fall in love with her, Nico. Wildly and desperately." She spoke the words as a curse. Lana's dark eyes glittered. "And I hope you'll suffer for the rest of your life when she never, ever loves you back."

"I'm so happy for you, Honora." Her maid of honor's voice was strangely wooden as she spoke the words.

Honora turned from the three-way mirror, where she stood in her simple strapless wedding dress in cream silk, which went to midcalf, and pretty sandals on her feet. Her toenail polish matched the bright pink roses in her long dark hair. A twenty-carat diamond—Nico had picked it out—was on her left hand.

She was standing with Emmie in a sunlit room inside Nico's Hamptons mansion. It was strange to Honora now, remembering how just a few weeks before she had rushed here on a stormy summer night, desperate to keep either Nico or her grandfather from being shot by his hunting rifle.

And now, Granddad had just returned from his honeymoon cruise with Phyllis yesterday, deliriously happy, and she herself was Nico's bride. She never could have imagined any of it.

With her grandfather so focused on his new wife, Honora had been glad that her best childhood friend, Emmie Swenson, had been able to take the weekend off to be here with her.

Unlike Honora, Emmie came from a large family. She'd grown up with her parents and four brothers, crammed into a tiny three-bedroom apartment on the same street. Also unlike Honora, Emmie had already worked her way through community college, sensibly ignoring her interest in baking to major in accounting. At twenty-five, her friend always looked exhausted, working long hours as an underpaid junior accountant on Wall Street, even on weekends.

And now, Emmie's round, pretty face looked more pinched than ever.

"You don't seem very happy," Honora said quietly.

Emmie took a deep breath. Her blond hair was tucked

back in a chignon, and she was wearing the strapless pink silk gown in a flattering bias cut that the wedding planner had arranged. "You're right." She rubbed her eyes. "I'm a lousy friend and I'm sorry." She looked at the door. "It's time to start. Your grandfather is probably waiting…"

"Wait." Honora looked at her friend anxiously. "Tell me what's bothering you."

Emmie paced a few steps, then stopped. "Look at how big this room is. And it's just a vacation home. For two people."

"Three, once we have the baby." Feeling guilty, Honora decided not to mention Nico's island in the Caribbean, his chalet in St. Moritz, or his recently acquired, but never lived in, villa on the Amalfi Coast, for which they'd leave tonight on their honeymoon.

Emmie looked out at the ocean through the wall of windows. "This is going to sound awful, but…for all these years, I've worked so hard." She sounded as if she were about to cry. "I've worked myself to the bone, doing a job I hate, with people who treat me like dirt. But I've done it because I want my family to have a better life."

"I understand, Emmie."

"How can you?" She looked from Honora, in her strapless silk wedding gown, to the bouquet of pink roses and the big diamond on her hand. "You didn't have to work for it. You're just *marrying* it."

Honora's cheeks went hot with shame as she looked down at her bouquet of pink roses. She couldn't answer because she knew everything her friend said was true. A lump rose in her throat.

"Damn it. I'm sorry." Emmie reached for her hand, tears streaming down her cheeks. "I hate myself for saying such awful things. And on your wedding day! I know you're not marrying Nico for his money. You love him." Her friend wiped her eyes. "You're lucky, that's all. And I'm hideously jealous and you should just smash cake in my face. I deserve it. Please forget everything I said and forgive me."

"There's nothing to forgive."

The two friends hugged each other, but as the wedding planner knocked on the door and said, "It's time," Honora still felt the distance between them. As they went into the hall, she felt like she was leaving the world she'd grown up in behind, the world where things made sense. Because Emmie was right. In what world was it fair that Honora was suddenly rich, just because she'd slept with Nico, while Emmie, who'd worked all these years at a job she hated, still had so little?

Things could have gone differently, Honora knew. If Nico hadn't insisted on taking responsibility, she'd be raising the baby alone, with very little income. In fact, that had been the most likely outcome. So Honora was lucky.

Just not lucky in love.

No, she wouldn't think about that. She'd just be grateful for what she had and not let herself feel sad about what she'd lost forever—the chance of loving someone, and being truly loved in return…

"Are you ready?" the wedding planner asked

brightly. Without waiting for an answer, the man turned to Emmie. "Now, you have to pay attention, when the music starts…"

"You look beautiful, Honora."

Turning, she saw her grandfather behind her in the hallway. He was dressed in a tuxedo, waiting to walk her down the makeshift aisle on the bluff outside.

"You clean up pretty well yourself." She was relieved to see him. Her grandfather would help steady her nerves, reassure her about the lifetime commitment she was about to make.

To her shock, she saw tears in his eyes. "I just wish your mother could be here."

Her mother. Honora had a sudden flash of memory of the day before the crash. Her red-haired mother, Bridget, hugging her tight. Holding her close.

I love you, Honora. You're all that matters. The light of my life. I love you.

It had been the last time she'd heard those words from anyone.

"No, don't," Honora gasped. She felt an ache in her throat that was as sharp as a knife. "Don't…don't make me cry. It'll…it'll wreck my makeup, and…the planner will yell and there will be a delay and cause everyone trouble."

Patrick glanced toward the wedding planner scornfully. "Huh. Let them wait." He leaned in close to his granddaughter and whispered, "Are you sure about this?"

She blinked hard to kill the tears and smoothed her face in a smile. "About what?"

"Do you love him, Honora? Nico? Your fella? Does he love you?"

Her smile dropped. She stared at him in shock. These were not questions she'd ever imagined her grandfather would ask. "You ask me this now? Right before the ceremony? After you were ready to shoot him with your rifle if he didn't marry me?"

Patrick shook his head, his bushy gray eyebrows furrowing. "I didn't understand it then." He ran a hand over his forehead. "After seventy-odd years on this earth, I didn't understand till now, how wonderful it can be to love the person you're married to. I didn't know." He looked up, his eyes gleaming with unshed tears. "Life's not just about duty, Honora. At least, it shouldn't be."

What? "But you said…"

"The last two weeks have been the best of my life. Don't wait until you're my age to learn about love. Don't make my mistake." He put his hand over hers. "If you don't love Nico Ferraro, if he doesn't love you, then don't do it. You come live with Phyllis and me. You and the baby both. As long as you need. It's your home, too."

Honora stared at him, stricken.

"It's time," the wedding planner trilled. "Maid of honor, go!"

"Honora?" her grandfather said urgently.

"Of course Nico loves me," she lied. "And I love him." She tried to smile. "Let's do this."

But as she held her grandfather's arm, and they went outside into the bright summer sunlight, she was suddenly afraid. Her grandfather's change of heart troubled her more than she'd thought possible.

Life's not just about duty, Honora. At least, it shouldn't be.

As they walked down the makeshift aisle between the folding chairs, on the grassy bluff overlooking the wide blue sea, she saw her friends and neighbors, the people she'd looked up to and loved her whole life. She saw Emmie's parents and her four strapping younger brothers crammed together, their shoulders overflowing the width of the folding chairs. She saw Phyllis beaming at Patrick, whose shoulders straightened a little as he walked by where his new bride was seated, and became visibly younger just at the sight of her.

Honora's footsteps faltered when she saw someone she hadn't expected—Lana Lee, Nico's famous movie-star ex, looking glamorous and insanely beautiful, and wearing big sunglasses in the back row.

You're so ordinary in comparison, her insecurity whispered. *Why would he ever love you if he couldn't even love her?*

"Steady," her grandfather said, holding her arm as he smiled at her. "We're almost there."

And then Honora saw Nico, standing beside a minister and his best man, whom she didn't know, beneath an arch of white and pink flowers. She felt the warm sea breeze and breathed in the scent of salt and green grass.

Her fiancé's dark eyes met hers. Above his sleek tuxedo, Nico's handsome face was shining, as if he'd never been happier. As if she were the most beautiful woman in the world. When she reached him, he took her hand.

Ten minutes later, he was kissing her as the minister presented them as husband and wife, to the guests' approving murmurs and applause.

Nico's kiss burned through her. And as Honora looked up into her husband's eyes, all her doubts were caught by the wind and blew out to sea. There was only him. Them. Forever.

CHAPTER SEVEN

WOULD THIS DAMNED reception ever end?

Nico didn't care about the wedding toasts—neither Emmie Swenson's sweet, tender good wishes, nor Theo Katrakis's surprisingly classy tribute.

"My assistant wrote it!" the Greek confided later, with a grin.

Nico wasn't hungry for the elegant beachside luncheon of lobster and asparagus in hollandaise sauce. He didn't want white wedding cake with raspberry filling. And the one thing that might have been palatable, the chilled champagne, he didn't touch, since Honora couldn't.

There was only one thing he actually wanted. And every minute he had to wait was agony.

Tables had been spread across the lawn with a view of the ocean. The July afternoon was bright, the sky a perfect blue. With only a hundred guests, the reception was intimate.

But not nearly intimate enough for him.

He looked down hungrily at Honora sitting beside him at the head table. Honora. Mrs. Ferraro. His wife.

She was leaning back against him in her wedding dress, her green eyes sparkling as she laughed at some joke Theo had made. The Greek was being his usual charming self, likely for the benefit of her maid of honor sitting on Honora's other side. But even still. Nico didn't like it, all that joy in her face, caused by another man.

He wanted his bride all to himself.

He'd never forget the moment he'd first seen her at the end of the aisle, in her strapless wedding dress, perfectly formfitting around her full breasts and baby bump, holding a small bouquet of pink roses. Her dark hair was falling free over her shoulders, and she had matching pink roses in her hair. Her green eyes had glowed as she walked toward him, holding her grandfather's arm.

Nico's knees had actually gone weak. He'd heard the thundering roar of the surf behind him as his blood rushed through his veins.

In that moment, everything else had fallen away. And he'd known she was the solution to that nameless emptiness, the anger, the restlessness he'd felt all his life. Once he possessed her, he would be whole.

Nico's voice had been calm and confident as he'd spoken his vows. Honora's had been quieter, seeming to hesitate, to tremble on the edges. But as the minister pronounced them husband and wife, and Nico took her in his arms and kissed her, he almost hated the applauding guests. He wished them a million miles away. He'd already waited weeks. Months. Years. In some ways, he'd waited his whole life. Now the hours of the obligatory wedding reception seemed unendurable.

The only good thing was that at least they didn't have to worry about an all-night spree of dancing and drinking, which the wedding planner had suggested but which he'd flatly refused, both because he'd promised Honora he wouldn't drink for the rest of her pregnancy, and because he thought he would explode if he had to wait to be alone with his bride until people toddled off drunk at two in the morning.

And they didn't have to worry about wedding presents, either. Honora had suggested that in lieu of gifts, guests could donate to their favorite charity. He'd been relieved. Nico hated receiving gifts—having to pretend to be grateful and indebted and say thank you and on and on, usually for some trinket he didn't value and had no use for. Charity was a fantastic idea.

Nico ground his teeth, trying his best to make it a smile as he looked around him at all the round tables filled with people who loved his wife. Why were they still here? It had been hours. The luncheon had been eaten, the cake served, the toasts given.

Too bad he didn't have the old man's hunting rifle. *That* would have encouraged their guests to leave right quick. His lips curved at the pleasant thought.

Then he sighed. As sensible a course as that seemed in his current state, he didn't think his wife would approve. Honora seemed to place a lot of importance on family, friends and community. Far too much.

But he wanted her to be happy. His arm tightened around her shoulders as she sat beside him at the head table. And soon, she'd make him very happy, too.

Honora looked up at him and smiled. "Don't you think?"

"He'll never admit it," Theo said.

He focused on them abruptly. "What?"

His new bride gave a dreamy smile. "I said I've never been so happy. I think we were meant to be. Soulmates. It was fate."

Nico blinked, then felt a sudden shock of panic that he couldn't explain. Just a moment before, he'd been thinking how contented he felt to be wed to her, how proud. But now he saw something in Honora's shining eyes, some overwhelming emotion that scared him. And he imagined he saw a question in her lovely face, wordlessly asking if he felt the same.

He didn't. His heart was a stone, had been since childhood. The only emotions he could still feel were anger and satisfaction and...anger. He felt satisfaction at the thought of possessing her, and winning his point, and bedding her, and starting a family with her.

But somehow he didn't think she would be flattered if he told her what was in his shallow heart.

Cover, block, hide.

Lifting her hand to his lips, he kissed it. "I think," he said huskily, "it is time for our guests to leave."

"Nico!" Honora blushed, but he saw how she hid a smile and felt the tremble of her hand in his own. That was enough. He rose to his feet.

"Thank you all so much for coming to our wedding," he said loudly, over the roar of the waves against the sand dunes. "But my wife..." *My wife!* What delicious words! "…is very tired, and so I'd like to invite you all to leave."

"Oh…" Honora moaned softly, covering her pink face with her hands. For a moment, the guests were silent. Then he received help from an unexpected source.

"Quite right," Patrick Burke said loudly, rising to his feet from the nearest table. The old man looked around at all the guests, almost entirely his and Honora's friends. "If we leave now, we can beat the traffic back to the city!"

Beat the traffic. Those were magic words. Everyone looked at each other with alarm and, as if of one accord, rose to their feet.

"May I take you back in my Bugatti, Miss Swenson?" Theo asked the maid of honor, Emmie.

"Not a chance," she responded crisply, then turned to hug Honora one last time. "Congratulations and good luck. You deserve everything good." She bit her lip. "And I'm sorry for…for what I said before."

"Nothing that wasn't true," Honora said, smiling, then handed her the bouquet of pink roses. "You're a good friend. The best. Thanks for being here for me."

"What was that all about?" Nico asked, as the guests crossed the grassy bluff back toward the sprawling mansion, back toward valet parking.

Honora watched them go, including her grandfather, who was holding Phyllis's hand tightly as they departed, and Emmie stumbling over the dunes with her family, and Theo, now flirting with Lana Lee.

Now *there* was an interesting idea for a couple, Nico

thought. Though they were so similar in their selfishness that they might kill each other.

"I feel bad…" Honora whispered, watching her maid of honor.

"About what?"

She turned back with a small smile. "Nothing."

"Good," he said, because the last thing he wanted to do was talk. Standing together on the grassy bluff, beside the flower-strewn wedding arch overlooking the vast blue-gray Atlantic, Nico pulled her into his arms.

"Kiss me, Mrs. Ferraro," he whispered.

Reaching up, she stood on her tiptoes and pressed her lips to his.

At her touch, something in his heart unfolded. His body relaxed and grew tight all at once. His hands moved in her dark hair, and pink rose petals whirled around them in the soft ocean breeze as she wrapped her arms around him, holding him close.

With an intake of breath, he lifted her up into his arms to carry her back to the house. Even at seven months pregnant, her weight felt negligible, as she pressed herself against him, so soft and warm. In this moment, he would have killed anyone who tried to take her away from him. Their eyes locked with wordless hunger as he carried her inside the sprawling beach-side mansion.

Inside, the back foyer was empty, deserted. The staff was gone. She looked around.

"Where is everyone?"

"I told Sebastian we wanted to be alone after the reception…to pack for the honeymoon. Bauer is waiting at the car." The Rolls-Royce had been festooned with flowers to take them to the airport. "We're due to leave in an hour."

"I'm so excited. I've never been to Italy." She gave a crooked smile. "The farthest I've ever traveled is New Jersey."

Nico wished she hadn't chosen the Amalfi Coast for their honeymoon. She'd said she wanted to see the country where he'd been born, but it only reminded him of unfinished business there.

Or maybe that was a good thing. Maybe this was fate, telling him to finally take what was rightfully his, the one thing his father had managed to keep from him: the palace where Nico's mother had once worked as a maid. His father's ancestral home, passed from generation to generation.

He'd tried to play nice. He'd offered to buy it from the widow for more than it was worth. His evil stepmother had turned him down flat.

Maybe it was time to play hardball.

"Nico?" She was looking at him with concern. "You were a million miles away."

Still holding her in his arms, he looked down with a reassuring smile. "It's nothing."

Honora looked around the enormous room with its tall windows overlooking the Atlantic. "All this space. Just for the two of us."

"Yes." He looked down at her in his arms. "I bought it hoping I'd someday have a family here. You've made that dream come true."

He felt her melt a little in his arms. Honora didn't

know that when he'd bought this house he'd imagined he'd have Lana Lee at his side, and he'd rub his success in the face of the man who'd callously let his mother die. The aristocratic father and stepmother who'd thought Nico wasn't *good enough* to be their son.

No. He didn't want to remember. That was all in the past. Stopping in the grand main room, he looked down at his wife, heavily pregnant, cradled in his arms. Honora was the future.

Standing in front of the tall, open windows, he felt the soft summer sea breeze coming up from the beach, swirling the long translucent curtains that were pushed back to the edges of the windows.

Kissing her, he gently set her down on her feet. She returned his embrace passionately. His hands roamed over her creamy wedding dress, cupping her breasts, her hips, her backside.

She drew back. "We can't," she breathed against his lips. "People will be waiting for us."

"We own the plane. Let the pilots wait."

"We could get caught, here in the living room…"

"The servants are gone. The house is all mine. Which means—" he kissed down her throat "—it's all yours…"

He heard the softness of her gasp as she leaned back to brace herself against a wall. She tilted back her head, her dark hair tumbling down her back in another flurry of pink petals.

He yanked off his tuxedo jacket, ripping off half the buttons of his white shirt in his desperation to remove it. She stroked the taut muscles of his bare chest, which was laced with dark hair. The feel of her hands on his skin made him ache with need.

She was pregnant with his child, and yet he felt as if he were touching her for the first time. As if this were his first time making love to anyone...

Reaching around her, he unzipped her wedding dress, and it fell to a heap at her feet. She stood before him like a goddess, her pregnant curves barely contained by a white demi-bra and tiny white panties. He swallowed.

"You're so beautiful," he whispered, touching her, stroking her. "I can't believe you're mine..."

He felt her shiver beneath his fingertips as he ran his hands over her arms, her shoulders, cupping her face as he kissed her hungrily, deeply. Her pregnant belly pressed against him. He wanted to ravish her, but he felt strangely uncertain.

He breathed against her skin, "I don't want to hurt you..."

She gave a shy smile that was the most seductive thing he'd ever seen. "You won't. Let me show you..."

She pushed him back against the sectional sofa in soft cream leather, at the center of the room. Climbing on top of him, she lowered her head to kiss him.

He felt the veil of her dark hair fall softly against his skin. Her hips swayed over his, causing his desire to spike higher still. With her on top, she was the one in control. He felt as if he were completely in her power.

It was a new sensation for him, and almost unbearably erotic.

Her full breasts overflowed the tiny silk bra. Reaching around her, he unhooked the fabric, allowing her swollen breasts to spring free. He gasped, then leaned up to suckle her, cupping both mounds with his hands. His hard shaft strained against his trousers as she straddled his hips.

She sucked in her breath, closing her eyes. For a moment she held still. Then her hips started to sway instinctively. The pleasure was too much. Ripping his mouth away from her swollen pink nipple, he gripped her wrists.

"No—stop," he gasped. "It's too much… I can't control…"

Her eyes flew open. She looked at him, her lovely face surprised. Then she smiled a small, feminine smile. In this moment she seemed far more experienced than he; she at least remembered the night they'd conceived their child. While he felt like a damned virgin, helpless, lost in his desire for her, this intoxicating woman who was now his wife.

Rising to her feet, she reached down and slowly unzipped his trousers, careful not to touch the part of him that most strained for her. She pulled the fabric, along with his silk boxer shorts, slowly down his legs.

Then, standing in front of him, she took off her white lace panties.

He closed his eyes, his breathing shallow and quick. Through the tall windows, the sea breeze blew against his hot skin as he felt her climb back over his naked body on the leather sofa. Naked.

He couldn't look. He was afraid if he did, he would explode. And he wanted to last for her. He should be able to last, damn it. With any other woman in his past, he'd always been able to last as long as he wanted. His sexual stamina was legendary.

But with Honora, he'd lost his power. He could not resist her. At any moment he knew he would surrender...

She lowered her soft naked body over his. She leaned forward to kiss his lips, and he felt the press of her pregnant belly, her full breasts against his chest, felt the whispered caress of her long hair. As she kissed him, a sigh came from the back of her throat.

And moving down, she lowered her naked hips to his, pulling him slowly, slowly inside her.

His lips parted in a silent gasp as his hands gripped the leather cushion beneath his body. He felt like he was hanging on by a thread.

Making love to Honora...

This woman he'd wanted for so long...

Pregnant with his child.

His wife.

All he could think of was her; he had to please her, to pleasure her.

His whole body was tense, on a razor's edge of desire.

Honora had never felt so wicked.

She was naked, in the middle of a grand room in a beach house, totally unprivate, where anyone in the open hallway could walk by—or someone outside could peer right into the enormous windows and see them, if they wanted.

But here she was, like a shameless wanton. It was only the second sexual experience of her life, but somehow, it felt different, as if their roles were reversed. She felt powerful, alive, with this billionaire playboy tycoon beneath her thighs, under her control.

Why did she feel this way? Because they were married? Because she was pregnant with his child? Or some other reason?

Her heart raced as she looked down at Nico's darkly handsome face, at his closed eyes, his rapt expression, as if what they were experiencing together was something wholly new, something holy.

And it was.

When they'd first slept together last Christmas, she'd been an untried girl, dreaming of a powerful man. Now she felt like she'd come into her own. She was a wife. A mother-to-be.

She was a woman.

Feeling him inside her, she felt pleasure burn through her body, from her scalp to her toes and everywhere in between. Gripping his powerful shoulders with her hands to support her weight, she lifted her hips, then lowered them again, drawing him inside her, deep, deeper still. His shaft was so wide, so hard and thick. He filled her deeper than she'd imagined. But he could not break her.

She heard him gasp, and he gripped her hips, stilling them.

"I can't, Honora. For the love of heaven—"

But seeing her power over him only increased her desire. When had she become so wicked? Was it the moment they were wed? Or had this passion always been inside her, waiting for the right moment—the right man—to set it free?

Leaning down, she kissed his mouth, licking his upper lip with a small flick of her tongue as he gasped her name.

Still gripping his shoulders, she slowly began to ride him. She closed her eyes as pleasure coiled deep inside her, tighter and tighter as her breasts bounced softly against her pregnant belly with each thrust. She held her breath as the tension built inside her, higher and higher. She dug her fingernails into his skin, going harder, faster, letting him stretch her wide, filling her to the hilt as her movements grew rough—

He gave a strangled curse and said her name as a prayer. "Honora!"

She exploded, soaring into the sky with a joyful cry, just as he poured into her with a guttural shout.

Afterward, she collapsed over him. They held each other, naked, on the white leather sectional, surrounded by tall windows, as the warm summer breeze oscillated the translucent curtains, caressing their skin.

Turning to her side, Honora rested her head on her husband's chest, listening to the beat of his heart as he softly stroked her hair, both of them sweaty and tangled in each other, the only sound the distant plaintive call of seagulls.

And it was in listening to his heart that she finally knew her own.

Her eyes flew open.

She was in love with him. Utterly, completely in love

with the man in her arms. The man who'd promised to be hers forever. The man who wanted to give her everything. His name. His fortune. His honor. His life.

Everything. Except his heart.

CHAPTER EIGHT

NICO HAD FLOWN the transatlantic route many times since he'd moved to New York and created his real estate development firm. He'd justified the expense of the state-of-the-art Gulfstream G650 because it gave him space and privacy, either to work in the sitting area, or to sleep in the private stateroom. Time was money.

The New York–Rome route had been the most frequent for the last two years, as he'd quietly bought everything his estranged father possessed, both assets and debts. After his father's death, he'd remained in Rome to distract himself with multiple billion-dollar deals, a new resort on the Costa Smeralda in Sardinia and other projects that were a quick flight away—Dubai, Athens, Barcelona.

He'd told himself there was no longer any point in trying to acquire his father's ancestral home, the Villa Caracciola, in the quaint village of Trevello on the Amalfi Coast. The former palace was decrepit, barely clinging to the rocky hillside. When his father's elderly widow, Princess Egidia, had still refused to sell it, even at top dollar, he'd let it go. Fine. Let her live there without staff and barely enough money to pay the electric bills. It seemed a just punishment.

But as he traveled back to the Amalfi Coast with his new bride, Nico found he'd changed his mind. Perhaps taking possession of the villa where his young mother had been seduced and betrayed would finally exorcise the ghosts of the past.

It wouldn't be the main goal of his honeymoon, of course. As they boarded the private jet in New York, all Nico could think about was making love to his wife. After their time together at the Hamptons house, he should have been satiated. Instead, he desired her even more. He was bewitched. *Obsessed*. Honora would be the main focus of this vacation.

But in spare moments, he would set his lawyers loose on his widowed stepmother, and force her to sell the Villa Caracciola. How hard could it be?

Once the jet was in the air, the smiling flight attendant served them a light meal of fruit and freshly baked crusty bread, cheese and ham, and sparkling water. As Nico and Honora ate, they looked at each other over the glossy oak table, and he felt shivery inside. By her dazzled expression, the way she bit her passion-bruised lips, he thought she must feel the same.

It was only the presence of the flight attendant, flirting with his security chief on the other side of the cabin, that kept Nico from sweeping all the food off the table and taking Honora right there. As it was, he barely tasted the food, and as soon as Honora was done their eyes met, and without a word, they rose and went to the private stateroom in the back.

Locking the door behind them, he kissed her passionately and drew her down to the bed. They remained there for the entire transatlantic flight, making love, sharing a shower in the tiny en suite bathroom—laughing at the tight squeeze of space. Holding each other quietly in bed afterward, they whispered the secrets of their hearts into the darkness.

At least, *Honora* whispered the secrets of her heart. How lonely she'd been as a child, how she'd never felt smart in school, how she'd always felt like a burden to her family.

Nico didn't answer. He just listened. Listened? He devoured and consumed her secrets like a miser tucking away pieces of gold. But he himself did not share. He'd learned long ago that being vulnerable was just offering rope for someone else to hang him with.

So he marveled at her fearlessness, as she confided that she'd never thought she deserved to be this happy, not after the way her parents had died in a car crash when she was a child. Somehow she seemed to think it was her fault—he didn't understand why, but he assumed she had her reasons. And he promised himself that he would never, ever use any of it against her.

Nico was her husband now. Her protector. If he could not love her, or feel emotions as she did, he could at least do one thing: keep her secrets as closely as he kept his own.

By the time the jet was preparing to land at a small airport near the Amalfi Coast, Nico was nearly licking his lips in anticipation of their honeymoon—two weeks of nothing to do but make love to his beautiful, sensual wife, showing her the pleasures of Italy, the delicious pasta and fresh seafood, and swim in the Tyrrhenian Sea.

And then, to cap it all off, in his spare time, he'd toss his wicked stepmother out of her rathole and raze the Villa Caracciola to the ground. In its place, he'd build a brand-new modern mansion in which to start his new dynasty.

He might have no idea how to be a parent, but he could for damn sure build his daughter a palace to live in. Whenever he felt anxious, wondering how on earth he would make his child feel loved when he himself had never known what that felt like, he reassured himself with the thought that his wife could be in charge of nurturing and loving.

Nico would be in charge of building an empire. He would protect and provide for them in a new ancestral home. The Villa Ferraro.

As he and Honora descended the steps of his private jet to the tarmac, it was full morning. The sun was warm, perfectly suited to his white collared shirt and dark trousers, and Honora's red cotton maternity sundress and sandals. Nico felt tired, having gotten very little sleep on the flight, but happy. What was it that made his wife so addictive, like a drug he could not resist?

And how was it possible that he'd barely noticed her for all those years? How had he never truly seen her until he'd been exhausted and drunk with a bad concussion last Christmas?

"We're here," Honora said, gripping the handrail as

she stood at the top of the steps, looking out rapturously at the tiny airport nestled behind the hills. *"Italy."*

He smiled down at her. It gave him so much pleasure to see the joy in her eyes. And at such a small thing—a honeymoon on the Amalfi Coast. He looked forward to a lifetime of seeing her lovely face light up with delight, knowing he was the one who'd put it there.

Not to mention a lifetime of nights where he made sure her full lips were bruised from the passion of his kisses.

As they came down the steps to the tarmac, with his security chief following, Nico saw Gianni, his personal assistant from the Rome office, holding a briefcase. Behind him, he saw a large SUV and a driver… Nico's mouth fell open.

"Welcome to Italy, sir." Benny Rossini, the young chauffeur he'd banished from New York City, smiled at Nico's new bride. "Honora."

Her face lit up. "Benny! You're here now?"

"Yes." He smiled. "I'm managing the new villa." He puffed up his chest a little. "A promotion. But I can still be your driver wherever you need to go." He gave a low laugh. "Driving along the Amalfi Coast is not for the fainthearted."

Nico scowled. When he'd told his residential staffing manager to move the young driver to another job, he'd never imagined he'd move Rossini *here*. He felt irritated. Really, Sergio should have known. He paid his staff well enough to expect them to read his mind.

It didn't matter, Nico told himself firmly. Honora was his wife now. Besides, they'd be at his estate for only two weeks. Surely he could endure his employee's presence for such a short time. And it wasn't like Rossini and Honora would be spending time alone together.

"Good to see you, Rossini," he said coldly, taking Honora's hand. As he helped her into the back of the luxury SUV, Nico added, without looking back, "Gianni, with me."

While his security chief, Frank Bauer, followed with their luggage in a separate vehicle, his assistant accompanied Nico into the back of the SUV, which had been fitted with two facing rows. Before the chauffeur even started the engine, Nico was speaking to his assistant in rapid Italian, telling him he wished to restart legal efforts to force the Villa Caracciola from the elderly widow's possession. Gianni seemed surprised, then moved forward, pulling up legal documents on his tablet.

Glancing up toward Benny Rossini, sitting in the driver's seat, Nico wondered whether he was listening. He didn't trust the young man, and the last thing he wanted was for his stepmother to be forewarned—or, for that matter, for Honora to hear a version of the story that might make Nico look like he was somehow the villain in this. Pressing the button to lift the privacy shield, he turned back to his assistant with a scowl, and told him in the same language that any delay was unacceptable. He wanted the Caracciola property *now*.

"Oh." Honora looked between the two men in dismay. "Are you planning to discuss business on the drive? In Italian?"

He saw how tired she looked, and was worried about

her and the baby. "Feel free to rest. The drive to my villa will take an hour."

She stared at him for a moment, then produced a sudden cheerful smile. "Don't worry. I'll just go sit in the front with Benny."

And before Nico could stop her, she hopped out of the back seat and went to sit with the young, handsome driver on the other side of the privacy screen.

As the SUV pulled away from the airport ten seconds later, Nico's assistant prattled on about how they could get around a governmental delay, which apparently was based on some claim that the widow's villa, two hundred years old, had "historical and architectural significance"—a classic stunt.

But he was distracted now. All he could think about was his wife, on the other side of the privacy screen, sitting beside Rossini, who was clearly infatuated with her, and though he had little money, perhaps the young man could offer her things Nico couldn't. Like emotion. Like vulnerability. Like love.

A curse went through Nico's mind.

"Sir? What do you think?" his assistant said in Italian into the sudden awkward silence.

Nico bared his teeth in a grin. "Just do whatever it takes to win."

His eyes strayed toward the closed privacy screen. He wondered what they were talking about. He wanted to lower the screen, but that would be an admission of jealousy, which he didn't want to make. He couldn't show Honora how important she was to him. That would give her too much power and make him feel...weak.

He had nothing to worry about, he told himself firmly. After all, it wasn't like his employee would be stupid enough to make a pass at his wife, with Nico himself sitting in the back of the SUV.

"I'm telling you, I'm in love with you!"

Sitting in the front seat, Honora drew back from the young driver, scandalized. "How can you say such a thing! I'm Nico's wife. I'm pregnant with his baby!"

Benny looked mournful, in a handsome, pudding-cheeked sort of way. He reminded her of a particularly forlorn basset hound. "I wish I'd only been brave enough to tell you before he seduced you…"

"Stop it!" As he started to reach his hand toward her, she slapped it away. "Watch the road!"

He did as he was told, gripping the steering wheel with both hands as they went around a taut hairpin curve on the cliff, practically dangling off the edge. It was a little terrifying, especially with her longtime phobia about car crashes. But not as awful as being pestered like this.

"And for your information," she added tartly, "Nico didn't seduce me. If anything, I seduced him!"

"No, that can't be…"

"It is," Honora said, exasperated. "He was drunk on Christmas Day, he'd just broken up with his girlfriend, and I took heartless advantage. So there!"

That wasn't exactly how it had happened, but she was fed up with Benny mooning after her.

The truth was, she'd been a little relieved when he'd been transferred to a different position in the Ferraro business empire. She felt sorry for him, and a little guilty, but she wanted him to be happy. When she'd come up here to sit beside him, she'd hoped to discover that the weeks and miles of distance, not to mention the fact of her marriage, had helped him gain a little perspective. She'd thought they could have a short private discussion that would put them both at ease.

But it had only made things worse. So much worse.

He was pale. "You're telling me I no longer have a chance?"

Honora wanted to scream. "You never had a chance with me! Never!"

He narrowed his eyes as he stared forward at the road. His expression was surly. "Because he's so rich, right?"

Her sympathy was disappearing. She was getting tired of friends, people who should have been on her side, implying she was some kind of gold digger.

"Because I'm in love with him." It was strange to realize that she was saying the words for the first time aloud, and not to Nico but to some other man who was stupidly making a pass at her.

His jaw dropped. "You can't!" He stared stonily at the road. "Nico Ferraro is a selfish bastard. He doesn't care for anyone but himself. And sooner or later—" he glanced at her "—he's going to hurt you. A man like that can do nothing else."

Honora felt a shiver of fear. Was Benny right? Would Nico break her heart and leave her crying and alone?

No. Impossible. He wouldn't leave her. He was the one who'd first wanted marriage, not her.

But you love him now, and he'll never love you back, whispered a small voice.

Setting her jaw, she pushed the painful thought away. "If this is how you show loyalty to Nico as your employer, and to me as a friend, I think you should seriously consider finding another job."

His lips twisted. "Way ahead of you."

Benny didn't speak to her again on the drive. Honora sat in the front seat, gripping the handle over her head as the big SUV swayed sharply around the turns of the narrow coastal road, passing within inches of tour buses flying in the opposite direction.

She felt sick from the twisty roads, exhausted by jet lag and lack of sleep, and horrified by his words.

But as the SUV finally entered through a guarded gate into a beautiful estate filled with lemon trees, Honora thought of how lucky she was: a newlywed, expecting a baby, in love with her husband. Surely she could be kind to Benny and not ruin his life just because of some ridiculous infatuation.

With a deep breath, she turned to him. "Look, I'm sorry. I don't want you to lose your job—"

"Don't worry about it." Pulling up in front of a grand, classical villa, he faced her. "I'll be fine. I already know someone looking for a driver. She lives in Hollywood." He gave a sharp smile. "I'll be a movie star within a year. I would have left a long time ago if you'd just been honest with me."

"When was I not honest?"

"Every time I flirted with you, showed you how much I liked you, bought you pickles. I believed you when you said you couldn't date because your grandfather needed you. But it was just an excuse. The second Ferraro crooked his finger, you couldn't wait to fling yourself into his bed. The second he bought that ring—" he eyeballed the huge diamond on her left hand "—you couldn't wait to say your vows."

Her cheeks went hot. "I didn't want to hurt your feelings…"

Benny gave a harsh laugh. "So you kept me around for years in hope, rather than telling a single hard truth to set me free."

"I never meant to—"

"Save it." Getting out of the SUV, Benny came around to her side and opened her door, his expression hard. He didn't look at her. Honora got out slowly, feeling bewildered by his sudden anger.

Wrenching open the rear passenger door, Benny waited stone-faced as Nico got out, his Italian assistant trailing behind him. Her husband looked between the driver and Honora sharply. He seemed to sense something was wrong.

As Frank Bauer got out of the second car, he called, "Hey, Benny, mind helping me with the bags?"

"Screw you, Bauer. And as for you—" Turning to Nico, Benny said something in Italian, complete with a gesture that even Honora knew was vulgar.

Nico's jaw dropped a little, but he responded with a cool smile, "Thanks for making this easy, Rossini."

"Same to you." Dropping the car key onto the gravel driveway, Benny stomped into the large, imposing villa, surrounded by gardens and overlooking the blue sea from a rocky cliff.

"Follow him," Nico drawled to his employees. "I imagine he's packing his things, but make sure he doesn't run off with the silver."

His security chief and assistant nodded, then hurried into the looming white villa with its elegant columns and statuary.

Nico's pretense of impassivity dropped as he went to Honora.

"What happened on the drive?" he demanded, looking down at her. "What did he say? Did he hurt you?"

"No, he just…he said he loved me. And he's angry because he thinks I led him on, but I didn't!"

"Of course not," he said soothingly. He gave a crooked grin. "You can't help it if you're desirable."

Honora choked out a laugh, but it sounded like a sob. "He'll be happier now. He's off for some new job, working for some woman in Hollywood." She tilted her head. "Do you think he's talking about Lana Lee?" Now *that* was a woman every man desired!

"Probably. I don't give a damn." His hands tightened at his sides. He turned grimly toward his villa. "I can't believe he tried to seduce you while I was in the same car. I'm going to go in there and—"

"No." Frightened by the look on Nico's face, she put her hand over his. "He didn't try to seduce me, not like you mean. And maybe he had a point."

"What do you mean?"

"All these years, I pretended not to notice how he was always flirting with me, asking me out to dinner."

"You should have just punched him in the face," Nico said darkly. She laughed, then saw he was serious. She shook her head.

"That probably would have hurt him less. I should have been brave enough to tell him the truth." Trying to change the subject and take away the scowl on her husband's face, Honora looked up at the enormous villa. "Wow. It's a palace."

Nico looked up at it. "It's not a palace. But it will do." His lips curved at the edges. "Until I get the one I *really* want."

"There's a villa nicer than this?"

"No. It's a ruin. And I'm going to knock it down and build something beautiful and new."

Shaking her head, she smiled. "You're never satisfied, are you?"

"No," he said huskily, drawing closer. "Especially not where you are concerned. I'll never get enough of you."

Her heart lifted, helping to dispel the dark clouds caused by Benny's words. *Sooner or later he's going to hurt you.* Glancing past his ear, she gave him a tentative smile. "Is that a garden?"

"Yes. I think you'll like it."

"Will I?" Holding his hand, Honora tugged him around the edge of the villa. She stopped, her mouth agape when she saw the formal garden with roses and palm trees surrounding marble fountains, and past that, groves of lemon trees with the biggest lemons she'd ever seen. Beyond the grand villa, she could see the turquoise sea crashing against the rocky cliffs. The soft Italian wind, redolent of oranges and spice, blew against her skin.

Nico looked down at her with a frown. "Are you crying?"

"I've never seen anything so beautiful," she whispered. She looked up at him. "I can't believe all this is yours."

He looked at her and his harsh expression changed, became almost tender, as a light entered his dark eyes. *"Ours."*

"Ours?" she breathed. "Even the garden?"

"No." He smiled. "The garden is just yours."

She danced on the spot. "I love you!"

Nico gave a surprised, joyful laugh as she threw her arms around him. He hugged her back.

Then she looked up at him, trembling with fear, and it felt as if time stopped. But she'd learned her lesson. It was better to reveal the truth, come what may.

"I mean it." With a deep breath, she looked straight into his eyes and said in a totally different tone, "I love you, Nico."

CHAPTER NINE

"I LOVE YOU."

Nico felt the words like a blow, as if she'd punched him in the throat.

I love you.

Those words had been said to him before, by over-eager girlfriends trying to take the sexual affair to the next level, to tie him down, to get him to put a ring on it. He'd seen them for the manipulations they were.

This was different.

Nico looked down at his beautiful pregnant wife in his arms. *Honora.* So beautiful inside and out. She meant the words. He saw emotion shining in her big green eyes. *Love.* What did that even mean?

Her heart-shaped face was filled with adoration—adoration Nico knew he didn't deserve. He knew he was selfish and ruthless and cold.

How had Honora convinced herself to see something else? Had he been complicit in her self-deception?

He also saw her unspoken longing for him to return her love.

Why? His demons reared their ugly heads. So she

could possess and control him? He would never allow himself to be so weak, so vulnerable, so helpless, giving his soul up into the power of another. As a boy, he'd always yearned desperately for attention, to feel like he belonged, like he was valuable. Instead, he'd been neglected, heartsick and alone, always wondering what was wrong with him that even his own mother seemed to regret his existence. *Never again.*

But as Honora looked up at him, as her soft body pressed against his, he looked down at her full breasts, pushing up against the thin straps of her red cotton sundress, and felt a different emotion. The only one he could allow himself to safely feel.

Desire.

Even after hours of making love to her—in the Hamptons, on the private jet—Nico suddenly wanted her more than ever.

She loved him. He'd never asked for her love, but now he possessed her, body and soul.

And if he couldn't love her back, he could at least give her his body, because it was utterly and completely hers…

The sky above the villa was bright blue, and a warm wind blew in from the azure sea as he held her amid the lemon groves. Nico saw the growing question in her beautiful face: Did he love her, too? He could not break her heart with the truth.

So he kissed her.

She felt warm in his arms, her baby bump pressed against him in her red sundress, as he stroked her bare arms. Her hands reached up to pull his head down to deepen the kiss, which made him ache for her even more. It was as close as he could get to love.

He ran his hands through her long dark hair, which swept loose and long over her bare shoulders. Her fingertips stroked lightly through his short black waves, then down over his shirt. Around them, he could smell the scent of lemons, of Italy, of the sea. He smelled roses and vanilla—the scent of his wife's perfume. He kissed her passionately, holding her close.

Cupping his unshaven cheek, she whispered against his lips, "I love you, Nico."

Again. He shuddered from a mixture of desire and dread. He liked her loving him, he realized. But if she knew he could never return her feelings…

He had to make sure she never realized that. For her sake. He had to protect his wife's feelings, to make sure she never knew his heart felt nothing.

But his body—

"I want you," he whispered huskily. He kissed her again and felt the sweet pleasure of her lips drawing him down, down into an intoxication more thrilling and mind-numbing than he'd ever experienced with alcohol. He felt her shiver in his arms.

Taking her hand, Nico pulled her away from the lemon groves, through the formal Italian garden, past the roses and burbling marble fountains. The warm sun caressed their skin as he drew her back to the enormous white wedding cake villa that was perched on a cliff overlooking the coast.

He paused for only a moment when he saw Benny Rossini scowling as he was escorted into a waiting SUV by his security chief. Honora watched, her face shadowed with worry and guilt.

Nico ground his teeth. Why would she feel guilty? Rossini himself was clearly to blame for his own bad judgment. But Honora's heart was so tender and kind that she blamed herself for everything.

"Make sure he gets his full salary for the month, and any vacation time owed," he told Frank Bauer, who nodded.

Honora turned to Nico. "I feel bad—"

"Didn't he say he was glad to go to Hollywood?" he said shortly. "He'll be fine."

"But—"

"Honora." As the SUV drove away, he looked directly into her eyes. "Why do you always blame yourself? It wasn't your fault. Let it go."

She bit her lip, then sighed. "Fine."

He pulled her inside the villa, and the tall oak door closed solidly behind them.

Inside, the two-hundred-year-old classical villa was elegant, stately in its age, and crowded with antiques, the antithesis of his sleek Hamptons beach mansion and stark Manhattan penthouse.

Honora looked with surprise at the foyer's checkered marble floor and frescoed ceilings of cherubs soaring high above. "This is…yours?"

He shrugged. "I bought it with the furniture intact."

Looking around, she gave an amused laugh. "This is the shack you're slumming in until you can buy the villa you *really* want?"

"Until I can build it. I told you. When I get my father's ancestral home, I will raze it to the ground and build something modern and new."

"An ancestral home?" She frowned. "That sounds important. Why not remodel and restore it?"

He looked away. "It's a symbol," he said quietly, "of everything my father did. The place where he seduced my mother, who was a maid in his house. Then he threw her out and refused to take responsibility for her pregnancy. He represents everything that's wrong and corrupt and cruel. I want to burn it all to the ground."

"Oh, Nico," she whispered. "I'm so sorry. No wonder you want to tear it down."

His eyes met hers. "I do. Then I will build a new villa. A new home. With you."

She seemed to visibly melt at his words. Emotion made her green eyes glow. At first it warmed him— but then his heart started to pound. *Danger!* He could not let himself feel emotion.

But desire…

Taking her hand, he pressed it to his lips. "I expect the Villa Caracciola to be mine within the week." He slowly kissed up her bare arm to her shoulder, feeling her shiver. "Until we can build our real home," he whispered, cupping her cheek as he slowly lowered his mouth to hers, "we'll just have to make do…"

Nico kissed her in the foyer until she sagged against him in surrender, both of them lost in pleasure. When he pulled away, he saw her beautiful face was dazed with desire. Taking her hand, he pulled her up the grand staircase.

He'd only visited this villa once, the previous November, when he'd bought it. He was relieved to find he still knew the way to the master suite. It was the only thing he'd refurbished, combining three bedrooms to make a single large modern one.

Huge windows and a balcony overlooked the picturesque sharp cliffs jutting into the turquoise sea. At the center of the room was an enormous bed. The white duvet was dotted with red rose petals. The marble fireplace had been filled with an enormous bouquet of pink and red long-stemmed roses. Nearby, an intimate table for two was covered with chocolate-dipped strawberries, sparkling pink lemonade, small canapés, fruit and tiny sandwiches.

Honora stopped, her sandals almost screeching to a halt on the hardwood floor, her eyes wide as her dark hair swayed over her red sundress. "What's this?"

Nico felt glad in this moment, so glad, that he'd taken the time to ask his Italian housekeeper to set it up. All so simple, and yet his wife looked more touched than when he'd dragged her to Cartier and insisted on buying her a twenty-carat diamond. She looked, in fact, as if she were about to cry.

Maybe he couldn't give her *love*. But romance, romance he could do.

"For you, my darling bride," Nico whispered. Coming forward, he cupped her cheek as he slowly lowered his lips to hers. "Roses and chocolates and kisses. Kisses most of all. Everything I have, everything I am…is yours."

Honora woke up smiling.

Late-afternoon sunshine was flooding through the

west-facing windows of their bedroom. She must have fallen asleep naked, she realized, after their lunch and lovemaking. She stretched languorously, loving every sweet ache of her body.

Every part of her felt touched by him, blessed. She didn't remember falling asleep, but then, she'd been tired even before they'd arrived at his villa, with all the passion they'd shared while crossing the Atlantic in his private jet, and before that in his Hamptons house.

Although, she knew Nico would say, if he were here, that it was *their* private jet. *Their* Hamptons beach house. *Their* Amalfi Coast villa.

But the thing she loved most about all of those places was that he was in them.

So where was Nico? Getting out of bed, she looked around her. Unlike the rest of the villa, which had been chock full of antiques, this gorgeous master bedroom was as sparse with furniture as Nico's other homes. Pulling on a silk robe that she'd bought in New York as part of the wedding trousseau he'd insisted on buying her, she peeked into the en suite bathroom.

It was gleaming, modern and new. And empty.

She glanced at the small clock over the bedroom's sleek marble fireplace, above the vase of long-stemmed pink and red roses. It was six o'clock. Almost dinner time, at least by American standards. And she was hungry. Being pregnant really gave her an appetite.

Or maybe she'd worked it up doing something else. Again and again. She blushed.

Taking a shower in the large walk-in shower, Honora relished the warmth against her skin as she scrubbed her hair. So much easier to do here than in that postage-stamp-sized shower on the private jet. Stepping out, she wrapped herself in a thick white cotton towel. As she wiped the steam off the mirror, she looked at herself in amazement as she brushed her teeth.

How had she stepped into this life? She didn't understand how she could be so lucky. What had she ever done to deserve it?

You didn't have to work for it. You're just marrying it.

Her smile fell a little as she remembered Emmie's bitter words, words her friend had apologized for and tried to take back. But it had never been about money for Honora. She would have been mad about Nico, rich or poor! She loved him just for himself!

She loved him. But did he love her?

Everything I have...everything I am...is yours.

Honora shivered, remembering how she'd felt when he'd kissed her earlier and taken her on that bed.

That meant love, didn't it?

Anyway, she didn't need him to say the words. He cared for her; he was committed to her. That was enough. Honora's heart could love enough for both of them. It *could.*

Getting dressed in a pretty, new cotton sundress, she pulled her hair back into a long ponytail and went downstairs.

After some aimless wandering along the villa's hallways, she finally found Nico in a home office with his assistant and several other men in suits, all of them speaking in tense, rapid Italian as they looked over papers spread across a large table. They looked up as she entered. Nico smiled.

"Honora. Did you enjoy your rest?"

Could his men guess why she'd so desperately needed one? She blushed. "Yes."

"I'm just getting some details ironed out for that real estate acquisition. You were asking to taste real Italian pasta, yes?"

"Yes?"

"As soon as I'm done here, I'll take you out to dinner in Trevello, if you'd like."

"Sounds lovely."

Nico's warm gaze traced slowly from her eyes to her lips, down her body to her sandals, leaving a trail of heat wherever they lingered. "I'm sorry I have business with my lawyers. I'll be done soon."

"I'll go wander the garden," she said, not wanting to be a bother.

The formal garden was even more lovely on closer viewing. Standing alone in the middle of the villa's perfect garden, with its spectacular view of the sea, she wished her grandfather could see these flowers. But he was busy with Phyllis, working in the flower shop, redecorating the Queens apartment. They'd decided to turn Honora's old bedroom into a home gym. "I gotta stay healthy to keep up with my wife," her grandfather had told her happily.

Honora looked out at the bright sun, lowering toward the sea. She was glad he was happy. She was, too. She was married and expecting a child.

So why did she suddenly feel so uncertain and alone?

"Stop it," she told herself aloud. "You have everything you could ever have wanted. More than you deserve."

She walked through the garden until it grew dark, then went inside to sit on the sofa outside Nico's home office with an old leather-bound book she'd found on the shelf of the library. By the time Nico shook her awake, it was hours later, nearly midnight.

"Sorry." He gave her a charming smile. "My lawyers took longer than I thought."

"That's all right," she said, rubbing her eyes, trying to wake herself up and be ready to eat dinner when her whole body said she should be sleeping. She felt totally upended by jet lag.

Outside the villa, there were streaks of velvety stars in the dark purple night. Helping her into his sports car, Nico drove her through the gate and out to the cliff road, twisting along the edge of the black Tyrrhenian Sea.

"The restaurant is just up there. The best pasta in Campania, which means the best in Italy, which, of course, means the best in the world."

But as he started to turn into the parking lot, a big RV coming from behind clipped the edge of his back bumper, causing the sports car to spin wildly through the gravel lot, rocking back and forth chaotically.

Their car spun toward the edge of the cliff.

Honora screamed. For an instant, she was eleven again, watching the whole world spin in front of her eyes. It was just like before. In selfishly asking for something she wanted, she'd ruined her life. Killed the people she loved most—

Nico gave a low, tense curse, gripping the wheel hard and forcing it to turn.

The car suddenly stopped. But her screaming didn't.

"Honora. *Cara*—"

She felt Nico's hand on her shoulder, heard his gentle voice. She opened her eyes and saw that the world had stopped spinning. Their car was still. Other than a cloud of dust around them, there was nothing to show that they'd nearly plummeted into the sea.

"I'm—sorry," she choked out. "I didn't mean to scream." Suddenly she was sobbing and his arms wrapped around her.

"It's all right." His voice was tender as he stroked her hair. "We were never in any danger, but I'm sorry you were scared." He looked fiercely behind them. "Damned tourists should know better than to try to drive this road in that thing."

Honora felt embarrassed, making such a fuss when they were trying to have a romantic evening. Pulling away, she wiped her tears. "I'm fine now."

"Are you sure?"

She nodded, avoiding his gaze. "Absolutely."

Opening her door, he helped her from the low-slung sports car and led her into a charming restaurant, which seemed very local. Perhaps because it was after midnight, the restaurant had no other customers. The owner was thrilled to see him. "Mr. Ferraro! I am so glad you are here!"

"*Grazie*, Luigi."

"My wife, she said you would come and bring your new American bride, your first night in Trevello. I said no, lovebirds have better things to do than eat! But my wife, she said, doing those things, one always gets hungry…"

"I can speak for myself," said his wife, who came over, smiling. She had an Australian accent. The two of them were good-looking and gray-haired, and Luigi pulled her into his arms, looking down at her lovingly.

"I will, and I do, and I should always listen to you." He kissed his wife's temple. "To listen as well as I love you, which is infinite and forever."

She looked up at her husband. Luigi abruptly cleared his throat, as if he'd just remembered they had customers. "So Peggy told me you called for a reservation…?"

"Yes. Um…" Nico had the grace to look sheepish as he clawed his hand through his dark hair. "I'm sorry we're so late."

The wife waved her hand, which was filled with menus. "That is no problem. We expected as much, seeing as it is your honeymoon. We are honored that you chose our restaurant for your first night." Escorting them to an amazing table by the window, with a view of the moon-swept sea, the lights of the village of Trevello and a flickering candle between them, she handed Honora a menu. "This is your first trip to Italy, *signora*?"

"Yes," she replied shyly. She looked at the menu, then said, "Nico says this is the best restaurant in all Italy, and as it is yours, will you please tell me what I should order?"

Luigi beamed at her, then plucked the menu from her hand. "You chose a good one, Signor Ferraro. *Signora*, I will be most pleased."

Fifteen minutes later, she was dismayed as they were served two full plates of portobello mushrooms sautéed with spinach in garlic and olive oil.

"Enjoy, *signora*!" he said.

"My favorite thing here," Nico said, and dug in.

Picking up her fork, Honora tried to smile. She cut very slowly with her knife, and she forced herself to take a bite.

"How do you like it?" Nico said, watching her.

"Delicious," she managed to say, trying not to breathe through her nose or taste the mushroom as she gulped it down.

He set his jaw. "Honora. If you don't like something, don't suffer in silence. Be honest. Speak up."

"I hate mushrooms," she blurted out. For a moment, she was shocked at herself, and even proud.

Then as she sat in the picturesque Italian restaurant with its amazing view, fear surged through her. What if Luigi's feelings were hurt by her honesty? What if her husband was embarrassed, or what if he despised her for not being sophisticated enough to enjoy this meal? Would he tell her he no longer wanted such an unpleasant wife who made such selfish demands?

Setting down her fork, she nervously lifted her gaze. Her husband smiled at her, his dark eyes glowing. Then he turned, lifting his hand for the restaurant owner's attention.

"Luigi. My wife doesn't care for mushrooms. Please get her something else."

"*Sì, signore*. But of course."

Nico's smile spread to a grin as he reached for her plate of mushrooms. "And I will take care of this."

Two hours later, they finished the most delicious seafood pasta Honora had ever tasted, along with crusty bread and Caprese salad with ripe tomatoes, basil leaves and fresh mozzarella laced with olive oil and balsamic vinegar. She felt happy, relieved. It was strange. Something about Nico made her feel brave, like she had the right to speak up for herself. Like she shouldn't take the blame for things that weren't her fault. Like she wasn't a burden, but a treasure.

Smiling, she drank creamy decaf coffee and finished a cannoli that was as sweet and light as air. Then her smile fell as she saw, on the other side of the empty cliff-side restaurant, Luigi tenderly kiss his wife. She saw his lips form the words *Ti amo.*

And just like that, all her happiness dissolved. Having told Nico that she loved him, she yearned so badly to hear those words back. How wonderful it would be to be loved, now and forever, after her hair had long turned to gray.

But why would she ever think she deserved to be loved like that, when—

She tried to push the thought away. But suddenly she couldn't.

"What's wrong?" Nico asked quietly. She looked at him, so handsome on the other side of the table, shadowed by the flickering light of the candle.

"I don't deserve this," she whispered. "Any of it. I never have."

"How can you say that? Of course you do. You're

the kindest person I know." He gave a grim smile. "If you don't deserve happiness, no one does."

"You don't really know me. What I did."

"So tell me." His voice was gentle.

Honora looked away. Through all the open-air windows, she could see the clusters of lights of Trevello's houses and shops, stretching joyously up from the sea to the sky, twinkling like stars.

"When our car almost went off the cliff, just because I wanted pasta…it all came back." She licked her lips, closing her eyes. "How I begged my parents to take me up to a pumpkin festival in the countryside, two hours outside the city. I thought if we could go, then maybe we'd be a happy family like in the ads."

"What happened?"

"My parents fought the whole time. Just like always. My mother cried and begged as my father drank and criticized her. He drank the whole time we were at the autumn fair, then crashed the rental car into an oncoming truck on the way home. The other driver lived. So did I." She looked up, her eyes filled with tears. "But my parents died because I just *had* to sit on a hay bale and eat pumpkin bread."

"No, *cara*." His voice was gentler than she'd ever heard as he put down his small cup of espresso. "They died because your father chose to drink while he was driving his family in a car. It wasn't your fault. You were a child."

Honora looked up at him, her heart pounding. Then she told him the worst. "They were miserable because of me. They only married because of me. Because I was born. They grew to hate each other. That was why she cried and he drank. They felt trapped but didn't know how to get out. Because of me."

He put his hand over hers on the table.

"It was not your fault," he said quietly. "Your parents made their own choices." He pulled away his hand, straightening his shoulders as he sat back in his chair. "Forget the pain they caused you. Be happy. Live your life only for yourself." He gave her a crooked grin. "That's what I do."

The thought was shocking to her.

"Live for myself?" she said. "But it's the people I love who give my life meaning. My grandfather. Our baby." Her eyes met his wistfully. "You."

A strange, stricken look came over Nico's face, and he abruptly looked away. In the flickering shadows of the restaurant, his jaw seemed hard enough to snap.

"Luigi, the check," he called. Turning back to her, Nico's expression was cold. "Your secrets are safe with me. I give you my word." Tossing his linen napkin down over the empty plate, he rose to his feet. "It's late. Are you ready to go?"

CHAPTER TEN

NICO HADN'T MEANT to hurt her.

Honora told herself that on their drive back to the villa beneath the moonlight, and as her husband made love to her in the darkness, and when she woke alone in bed the next morning. She heard the birds singing in the palm trees overlooking the turquoise sea and repeated it again. He hadn't meant to hurt her.

She'd poured out the most agonizing secrets of her heart, the deepest burdens she carried—that her existence had caused her parents' misery, and her selfish desire to go to a pumpkin festival because of the absurd idea that it would bring them together as a family had caused her parents' deaths.

And all he'd said was that he wouldn't tell anyone. *Your secrets are safe with me. I give you my word.* As if her fears were not only true but shameful, and that if anyone else knew, they would despise her.

Be happy, he'd said. *Live your life only for yourself. That's what I do.*

Nico was living his life only for himself?

What did that even *mean*?

Over the first few days of their honeymoon, Nico worked only in the mornings, and arranged for them to take excursions together in the afternoon. They traveled via helicopter to Rome, and had private tours of the Colosseum and St. Peter's Square. As they wandered the Roman Forum and tossed a coin in the Trevi Fountain, Honora was filled with wonder and delight, seeing things she'd only dreamed of as a teenager growing up in Queens. And she found herself telling her husband all kinds of stories about growing up in her neighborhood, her friends, her love of books, her interest in flowers and plants. "I had no choice about that," she'd added, laughing, "spending time with Granddad!"

Later, wandering with Nico through the gardens of the Villa Borghese, she talked at length about the best way to care for cypress and pine trees and keep aphids away from roses. She was a little embarrassed later, but it was hard not to talk. Nico was a very good listener.

The next afternoon, he took her to Pompeii. The Roman ruins were remarkable, but seeing where all those people, those *families*, had died suddenly in the eruption of Vesuvius two thousand years before, she became mournful. Nico lifted her spirits afterward by taking her to the most famous pizzeria in nearby Naples, where they shared a margherita pizza with basil and tomato sauce, mozzarella cheese oozing over a crust that was as light as air. As they sat at a small table, surrounded by the hustle and bustle of other customers, she found herself telling him about the disastrous time she'd tried to make pasta from scratch. "Even the neighbor's dog wouldn't eat it," she said with a laugh.

None of her stories were earth-shattering, but it was all of them together that made Honora who she was, so she decided not to be embarrassed. She was glad to share her life with the man she loved. Both afternoons were wonderful and warm, and she loved feeling her husband's presence, whether she was sitting beside him in the helicopter or encircled in his arms in the back of the sedan, chauffeured by Bauer.

It was only much later, after they'd returned to the Amalfi Coast, that it occurred to Honora that she'd done all the talking. Nico was a very good listener, but he'd told her almost nothing about himself, about his own stories and hopes and dreams. The closest he'd gotten was when she'd said in the Pantheon, "You were born here, weren't you? I'd love to see where you grew up."

"Now *that* is ancient history," Nico had said lightly. Then, with a careless smile, he'd distracted her, pointing out the concrete dome, which was apparently special for some reason. And he'd never brought up the subject of his past again.

Looking back, the golden glow of happiness seemed to lose some of its shine.

Honora wanted so desperately for them to be happy. They had everything anyone could want on this Italian honeymoon in this luxurious villa, their baby expected soon. So why did Honora feel like something wasn't right? Something was…missing, and it made her feel empty.

As the first week of their honeymoon passed, then the second, there were no more fun excursions. She watched with mounting dismay as, every day, Nico disappeared into his home office with an increasing number of lawyers and staff. He was apparently having some trouble closing the deal for the Villa Caracciola. Feeling lonely during the second week, she'd once tried to join them. Nico had all but blocked the door.

"I'm sure you have more enjoyable things to do," he'd told her firmly. He handed her two platinum credit cards. "Go shopping down in the village. Or Bauer can drive you if you wish to see Sorrento or Positano."

"Without you?"

He glanced at his lawyers grimly. "I'll be done in an hour or two. Then I'll join you."

But the hour or two was always eight or ten or even, yesterday, twelve. Honora entertained herself by spending time in the villa's delightful formal garden, walking among the flowers. It was perfect in its ornate simplicity, but, she thought, if she were going to design a garden, she would make it more random, wilder. But the gardener clearly didn't need her help, and he didn't speak English beyond smiling at her and bringing fresh flowers into the villa every day—mostly roses.

She got to know the other staff at the villa and learned some basic greetings and questions in Italian. The housekeeper, Luisa, had a little white dog who needed daily walks, and so when the older woman twisted her foot a few days after they arrived, Honora happily offered to take Figaro outside in her stead.

Taking the dog down the steep hillside to the village that clung to the rocky shores that rose sharply from the sea, Honora walked through Trevello alone. For a honeymoon, she thought, it was surprisingly lonesome.

In spite of the amazing sex every night, for which Nico still always found time, Honora was almost relieved when the two weeks finally came to an end. It wasn't so enjoyable to eat delicious meals alone, or sit in the villa alone, or walk along the coastal road alone. She yearned to go home to her grandfather and friends.

Then, the night before they were supposed to leave, Nico suddenly announced that they'd be staying in Italy "indefinitely."

Honora said anxiously, "How long?"

"As long as it takes for me to buy the villa," he bit out. When she flinched at his angry tone, he tried to smile. "On the plus side, it will give us more time in my birth country, so I have decided to host a reception here, to properly introduce you to all my European friends. We'll have music, and dancing…"

Her old insecurity went through her. "You want to introduce me? At a formal ball? To a bunch of wealthy, gorgeous society people?"

"As you said, such social events are necessary, are they not? For the community?"

"I guess so," she said reluctantly.

"The household staff will plan everything. All you need to do is find a ball gown. Excuse me." He glanced back at his home office, which was filled with even more lawyers than before. "I must get back to work."

She didn't ask questions because she feared he'd only snap at her. She wanted to be supportive, to be a good wife. Surely if she was always agreeable and kind, he would love her for it? Surely she should be as small and quiet as she could, no trouble at all, so she wouldn't be a burden?

She'd done that most of her life. She told herself she could do it again.

But suddenly, strangely, she didn't want to. She thought of how she'd felt so powerful in Nico's bed. How he'd encouraged her to stand up for herself, in everything from not feeling guilty over things that weren't her fault, to refusing to eat things she didn't like.

Be happy. Live your life only for yourself.

Okay, she thought, *I'll give it a try.*

So the next day, when Honora walked the dog, she didn't rush right back to the villa in case her husband finished work and wanted to see her. No. She would try to make herself happy.

She took the long coastal path and looked out at the sea.

She could see Le Sirenuse in the distance, the three lonely islands rising from the blue waves. One of the villa's staff members had told her that, according to ancient legend, the rocks had once been inhabited by sirens who'd seduced sailors to their own destruction.

Honora shivered as she looked at the three rocky islands in the distance. How awful to think that someone could be led to their own ruin, simply by following their heart's desire.

It felt good to be out of the villa, and not just falling asleep in a chair with a book in her lap, waiting for her husband to have time for her. Honora felt exhilarated to be in this village, to breathe this air, sweet with lemons and salty from the sea, that seemed so different from New York, or even the Hamptons.

As the days passed, she started talking to people and making friends. Once she tried it, she found it wasn't even hard. Many English-speaking tourists came to the Amalfi Coast, and Trevello's shopkeepers and inhabitants all spoke English to varying degrees, enabling her to chat with everyone, usually about the sweet-natured dog Figaro, who attracted love everywhere.

As the housekeeper rested her twisted ankle, Honora looked forward to walking her dog every day, hiking along the cliff-side path, even window-shopping in Trevello, looking for a ball gown.

Early morning was the best time to walk, she found, before floods of tourists arrived via buses or cruise ships. When the town was quiet, she could walk Figaro and hear his nails click against the cobblestones, as church bells echoed and shopkeepers swept their doorways and restaurant owners sprayed off their patios. She saw elderly women heading to church—stoop-shouldered, with handkerchiefs covering their hair—while other women of a similar age snuck back furtively to their homes, returning from midnight assignations, chic in Dolce & Gabbana and navigating the crooked streets in high heels.

She loved Italy!

Honora met an older lady of the first type coming up the hillside early one morning, pulling a small wheeled basket filled with groceries. She seemed to be struggling to lift it over the crooked curb in front of a tall gate and stone wall.

Honora hurried forward, Figaro trotting on his leash behind her, his tongue lolling happily. "Please, let me help," she said awkwardly in English, hoping the woman wouldn't think she was trying to steal her grocery basket.

The elderly woman smiled at her sheepishly. "*Grazie*. It is not so easy anymore." She looked at Honora's belly. "But you should not be lifting things…"

"I'm fine." She tilted her head, looking up at the large, decrepit villa above them on the cliff. "Do you work up there?"

She gave a low laugh. "It is worse than that. It is mine." She paused as a sad expression crossed her face. "For now…"

"Are you moving? That's a pity. Trevello is so lovely."

"I wouldn't leave by choice." The elderly woman looked down at her wrinkled hands. "Someone is trying to force me from my home."

"That's horrible!" Honora was indignant. "There ought to be a law!"

She helped the woman pull the heavy groceries past the gate and up the long, winding steps toward her faded house. It was not an easy journey. Even Figaro looked tired by the time they made it all the way up the many steep steps.

As Honora bid the elderly woman farewell, it crossed her mind that she'd ask their housekeeper if something could be done for her. Perhaps to have her groceries delivered?

Poor old lady with no family to take care of her, and her awful stepson trying to steal her home. When

Honora had asked why her family didn't help, she'd learned that the woman's children had died when they were babies. Pregnant as Honora was, her heart broke even more.

After that, she made sure to check on her every day, just to say hello, but mostly to make sure the sweet old lady didn't break her leg trying to haul groceries up alone.

But one such morning, after nearly four weeks in Italy, changed everything.

It had started out so well. The proprietor of one of the little shops had found Honora the ball gown of her dreams, handmade in Naples by his cousin, who'd come that morning to do the final touches on the fit. Her belly was huge now, she had to concede. As she left the shop, the owner and his cousin promised to have the dress delivered to the villa. Just in time too, because their formal reception was *tomorrow*.

Walking back up the cobblestoned road, the dog bounding happily behind her, Honora hummed happily to herself. Her husband had promised, absolutely *sworn*, that he'd finalize his business that afternoon. Apparently his acquisition of the Villa Caracciola was on the verge of a breakthrough. His team of lawyers had cracked the current owner's legal objections, apparently by some unorthodox means.

"Unorthodox?" she'd asked.

"Don't worry about it," he'd replied, smiling. "It just means we're going to win."

To celebrate, he was going to sail with her on his yacht to the isle of Capri. She was already dressed for the excursion, in maternity capri pants, a white bateau T-shirt, with a red scarf wrapped around her dark hair.

So after tomorrow night's formal reception, they'd be able to go home to New York. *Finally*. Her baby's due date was growing perilously close, less than a month away. She'd started visiting a doctor in Positano for checkups, just in case, but she wanted to be back in New York when she gave birth. Her grandfather kept sending messages, asking when she was coming home.

Honora blinked herself out of her thoughts when she saw the elderly woman, Egidia, standing outside her gate in Trevello, looking around anxiously. As soon as she saw Honora, with Figaro beside her, the woman blurted out, "Is it true your husband is Nico Ferraro?"

"Yes." She smiled. "Do you know him?"

The white-haired woman's face crumpled. "He is the one who is taking my home…"

Then she'd told Honora a story she'd hardly been able to believe. One she kept thinking about, over and again, for the rest of her dazed walk home.

"There you are," Nico said when she finally came inside. "Where have you been all this time?"

"Out." Squatting down, she let Figaro off his leash, and the little dog raced back to the kitchen.

Nico's forehead furrowed. He seemed confused by her cold tone, as well he should be—he'd never heard it before. "Are you ready to go for a little adventure?"

"Yes," she said quietly, feeling like she'd already had more adventure than she could stand. As she looked at Nico in the checkered hallway of the elegant villa, it was as if she were seeing him for the first time. He was darkly handsome, wearing a blue shirt with the top two buttons undone. His body was so powerful, his shoulders broad. She'd kissed every inch of his skin, as he had hers.

She'd thought she knew him. She'd only known the man she'd wanted him to be.

Frowning at her unusual reserve, he looked her over from her sandals to her capri pants, to the red scarf in her hair, then bent to kiss her on the cheek. "You look beautiful. Were you shopping in Trevello again?"

"I found a gown for the reception." She tilted her head. "I was walking Figaro. And talking to people in the village," she mumbled.

"Figaro?"

Did he really not know? "Luisa twisted her ankle a few weeks ago. Tripped on a stepstool. He's her dog. You haven't noticed her hobbling around the kitchen on crutches?"

Nico looked at her in surprise. "Is she? I didn't notice." He nuzzled her. "I should bring you to work for me," he said lazily. "You're better than a bloodhound. We'd get our deals done faster, and probably cheaper, too, if we knew everyone's secrets."

Honora stiffened. "It's not about ferreting out secrets. It just helps to know what people are going through."

"Helps what?"

"To know how to be kind, and comfort them through it."

Nico barked out a laugh, then sobered when he saw she was serious. Looking away, he said in a low voice,

"I'm sorry. I just learned to see people's secrets differently."

"As weapons?"

He gave a brief nod. "In business, if you know your rival's priorities—or better yet, their guilty secrets—it's very useful. If you know someone is running out of cash, you can get them to drop their price because they're desperate. If you know secrets about their banker, their lawyer, you can convince them to do a shoddy job for their employer. If you—"

"I get it." Feeling sick, Honora looked at her husband in the grand foyer of the Italian villa. "So that's what you do? Blackmail people? Hurt them?"

"Blackmail?" Nico looked at her incredulously. "What do you think this is? Real estate isn't about making friends. It's a battle. If I'm disciplined, I win. If I'm not, if I'm weak, I'll be the one who's destroyed."

"You see sharing as weakness," she said slowly. "That's why when I told you about my parents, you said my secrets were safe with you."

He straightened. "I want you to feel safe. To know I'm on your side. I will never let anyone hurt you, Honora."

What about when he was the one who hurt her? she thought.

She was quiet as he drove them to the marina, where they boarded his yacht, the *Lucky Bastard*. She felt Nico's gaze, his full attention. But what she'd learned that morning hung like a dark cloud over the distant horizon.

Maybe Nico was right about knowledge being a

weapon, she thought. Because what she'd heard about him from Egidia Caracciola felt like a bullet wound in her heart.

She had to confront him about it, but she feared she already knew what his reaction would be. And if she was right, their marriage might come crashing to the ground. She was afraid it would be the end of everything, because how could she spend the rest of her life with someone so heartless and cold?

The yacht crossed the Tyrrhenian Sea to Capri, the legendary playground for the wealthy just off the Italian coast. Around them, the yacht's staff bustled about, offering sparkling water and fruit, delicious meats and cheeses and freshly baked bread.

But for once, Honora had no appetite.

Nico remained close at her side, touching her hand, being charming, pointing out the sights—particularly the three rocky islands she'd looked at from a distance. "Le Sirenuse," he said. "Also called Li Galli. There's a story about sirens, luring lovestruck sailors to their doom…"

"I know," she said flatly. She felt tears burning the backs of her eyes and blinked fast, looking out at the bright blue horizon. As the yacht skimmed lightly over the water, the beautiful isle of Capri loomed large, and she knew she wouldn't be able to squelch her emotions for much longer. She turned her face to the sun and closed her eyes.

What else hadn't he told her?

Who *was* Nico Ferraro?

"Is everything all right, *cara*?" he asked in a low voice. Blinking, she tried to smile.

"Of course." But the words caught in her throat.

He clearly intended to make this afternoon special and romantic. When they arrived at the marina, he was quick to grab her red scarf when it got tugged away from her dark hair by the wind. Holding her hand, he helped her off the gangplank of the ship and along the dock into the charming seaside village. And he didn't let go of her hand.

As they explored the island together on foot, he was attentive, warm, sweet. But that only made her feel sadder as they wandered in and out of tiny shops, including, at his insistence, the fancy designer boutiques and jewelry stores that filled this exclusive, dreamy island.

Honora preferred the quaint little tourist shops. Trying to avoid his direct gaze, she bought some Limoncello liqueur and gardening gloves for her grandfather, some *cioccolato al limone* for Phyllis and a hoodie and snow globe for Emmie.

"All these gifts for others," her husband murmured, looking down at her, cupping her cheek. "I want to get something for you." He put his large hand gently on her belly. "What do they call it? A push present? I want to get you the best push present in the world, so if you go through pain giving birth to our child, you won't feel it, but you'll only remember the reward."

Honora looked at him, then said in a strangled voice, "*Our baby* is the reward."

His expression changed. "Of course. But I also want to get you a gift. Just for you." He grinned. "Think of it as recompense for all these weeks when I was so distracted."

He thought people's secrets were weapons to be used against them—even against his own family. He thought Honora wanted to get paid for giving birth to their child. He thought he could make up for his absence during their honeymoon by throwing money at her. All of it was adding up in strange ways. She swallowed hard.

"Are you hungry?" he asked. "It's early, but you didn't eat much lunch…"

"If you want," she said, still not meeting his eyes.

They ate dinner at a taverna on the edge of the sea, where she didn't even taste her *linguine con vongole*, and the conversation was stilted. She could feel his bewilderment, that even though he was trying so hard to please her, somehow, it wasn't working.

They finally returned to the yacht at twilight, and sailed back across the sea as the red and orange sun fell into the western horizon.

He pulled her beside the railing, where the staff couldn't hear. "What's going on, Honora?"

"Why do you think something's going on?" she said, evading him.

Nico looked down at her, so darkly handsome that her heart twisted in her chest. "I wanted today to be special. I hoped to buy you a gift you could treasure…"

Feeling the ache in her throat, she looked away at the dark glittering sea. "The gifts I treasure aren't things you can buy."

"Oh, come on," he said, trying to tease her. "A diamond tiara? Your own yacht? A green Ferrari to match your eyes?"

She said in a low voice, "That's not what I care about."

"What is it, then?" Red twilight was turning violet across the Tyrrhenian Sea as he looked down at her grimly. "Tell me what's wrong, Honora."

She took a deep breath.

"I want you to tell me why you're trying to hurt people. And don't tell me it has anything to do with business." She looked him in the eyes. "Why are you trying to destroy your own family?"

After all their days apart, Nico had wanted today to be special. He'd wanted to romance her, if he could not love her.

After weeks of frustration, his lawyers had finally found a way to force the sale of his father's ancestral home. Nico's stepmother had been vicious, keeping the villa tight in her grip, using every trick she could, calling in favors from old friends in law and government, even pulling in environmental and architectural objections. In the last month, Nico had spent millions of euros in legal fees, far more than the property was actually worth.

But now, finally Villa Caracciola would be his. His stepmother was out of money and out of options. The villa was her only asset. She had no choice.

It had been a long, hard fight, but it was nearly over.

Through it all, Nico had missed being able to enjoy his wife's company, since he'd seen her only at night, in the dark heat of their bed. He'd never intended for her to spend the days of their honeymoon alone, or for their time here to stretch to a month. But as he'd told her, real estate was a war, and this was one battle he did not intend to lose.

Now, he was eager to make up for lost time with Honora, with some grand gesture to delight her. And what better place than the famously romantic island of Capri?

Sailing across the sea in their yacht and walking the charming streets hand in hand with his beautiful wife— so lovely in her white T-shirt showing off her curves, and the red scarf pulling back her long, tumbling dark hair—should have been the most perfect day of their honeymoon.

Instead, the day had been useless. Honora, usually so loving and warm, had refused to even *look* at him.

Now, out of the blue, she'd attacked him like this.

Nico pulled away from her on the yacht's railing, feeling strangely hurt. He didn't understand what she was talking about, but he felt her harsh criticism, just when he'd least expected it.

"Trying to destroy my family?" he repeated, blinking in the twilight. "What are you talking about?"

"You never told me you had a stepmother!"

"Are you kidding? *Her? She's* not family."

"Of course she is." She lifted her chin. "No wonder you bought a villa so close to Trevello. You said you were going to knock down your father's ancestral home. You neglected to mention someone was still living in it—a sweet old lady!"

"Sweet old—" He stared at her, speechless. "You've got to be kidding. That woman is horrible. A snooty aristocrat who believes she's better than everyone else."

"If you ask me, you're the one who thinks you're better," she said coldly. "You make your own rules. You want what you want, and don't give a damn who gets hurt while you get it."

Nico stared at her, feeling sick as he stood on the deck of his yacht in the fading purple twilight. Honora's lovely eyes were hostile and angry—the eyes of an enemy. In his home. In his yacht. With his name. Carrying his baby inside her.

Beneath his feet, he could feel the sway of the waves unsettling him, making him feel like at any moment he could get knocked down.

How had it happened that his sweet, kind wife, the woman he'd thought would never challenge him or work against him, was hurling accusations from the same sensual lips he'd kissed so passionately?

"You don't know what you're talking about," he said in a low voice. "Egidia Caracciola is not some gentle, helpless old lady."

"No? She can't even carry her own groceries, and you're trying to drive her from her home without a cent!"

"It's not my fault my father left her a pile of debts."

Honora lifted her chin. Her green eyes glittered in the red sunset. "It *is* your fault, Nico, and you know it. You gathered up all his debts and then demanded that he pay them all in full at once. As his creditors never would have done."

"So what are you saying? That I killed him? That I caused his heart attack? You're doing her dirty work, Honora—using the very words she insulted me with, over his grave."

"She was probably upset, lashing out—"

"I'm the one who should be lashing out. Did you know I called my father after my mother's cancer diagnosis?" His heart was pounding, flooded with emotion he didn't want to feel. "The only time I ever asked him for anything. I begged for money to try to pay for an experimental treatment, and he refused. He said we were nothing to him. And she died."

Her expression changed. She whispered, "Maybe he didn't have the money…"

Nico looked away. "He was rich back then. He just didn't care. So I promised myself that someday I'd show him how it feels, to be desperate and poor and to ask your own blood for help, only to have the door slammed in your face."

"He hurt you," Honora said quietly.

"Yes."

"You've spent your whole life trying to get revenge."

"Yes."

"But your father is dead." She lifted her chin. "Why are you punishing *her*?"

When she put it like that, it did seem strange that Nico would go to such obsessive lengths to get revenge on an elderly woman he'd met only twice in his life. After all, he couldn't blame Egidia for his mother's death—at least not directly.

And yet something in his heart yearned to get the

woman's attention, since he could no longer get his father's. He wanted to force his father's wife to admit she'd been wrong, and that she was sorry. So very, very sorry.

He set his jaw. "What do you know about her?"

"I met her a few weeks ago in Trevello while I was walking the dog. I helped her carry some groceries, and this morning she realized who I was."

He set his jaw. "She was probably targeting you all along, as a soft touch to try to get to me."

"No. She wasn't." She glared at him. "She has almost nothing, but you're trying to take her house."

"I did offer to pay her for it. It's not my fault she's forced me to play hardball."

"Is that what you call it? You didn't even *try* to go to court to legally claim your father's estate. He had no other children. That would have been kinder. No, instead you slowly ruined him, *humiliated* him, as you're now doing to her."

"You think I'd want to claim Arnaldo as a father after he rejected me? No. He made me a stranger so I'm taking his estate like a stranger. By force."

"And what about Egidia? His devoted wife of fifty years?"

Devoted. Nico realized he was trembling. "I don't give a damn. She's nothing to me."

His wife stared at him for a long moment in the darkness as their yacht approached the glittering lights of the Trevello marina. "You're lying. You *hate* her. Why? What did she ever do to you?"

Honora was right, Nico suddenly realized. He did

hate Egidia Caracciola. With a passion. Gripping the railing, he turned away.

"I saw her with my father once, on the street in Rome. I was just seven years old. My mother pushed me forward, begged Arnaldo to recognize me as his son. Egidia wouldn't let him even *look* at me. She couldn't admit her husband had a bastard son. Because of her pride."

"Or maybe she was distracted with her own grief. She lost three sons of her own. Did you ever think of that?"

Nico blinked, turning to her. "What are you talking about?"

"I asked her why she was living alone in that old mansion with no one to help her. She said long before she lost her husband, she'd lost their three children as babies, one by one." Wrapping her hands protectively over her baby bump, Honora whispered, "Can you even imagine? Three?"

He stared at her, his heart pounding. Then he pushed away what was obviously an attempt at emotional manipulation. "She probably made it up. To try to get sympathy."

"How can you be so cold? Just go talk to her!"

"No." Nico's voice was like ice. The sunset that had been so vibrant and bright had turned dark shades of bruises and blood, and the sea now seemed deathly black. "Put her from your mind. She's not family. You are." He set his jaw, clenching his hands at his sides. "Don't let her drive a wedge between us, Honora. Do you want to be my wife?"

She sucked in her breath. "Now you're threatening to leave me?"

"I'm simply stating a fact." Nico looked at her, and felt nothing. "Either you're with me, or you're against me. You must choose."

"I choose you," she choked out. "Of course I do."

He hadn't realized he was holding his breath until he exhaled. He held out his arms, and after a brief hesitation, she walked into his embrace, leaning her cheek against his heart.

But as he stroked her hair, Nico had the unsettling feeling that something had changed between them.

His sweet wife had betrayed him, attacking him without warning. He would have to be on his guard from now on. Raise walls to protect himself. Make sure he didn't feel too much. Stay distant. Stay numb.

Because Nico would never let anyone hurt him, ever again. Not even her.

CHAPTER ELEVEN

THE NEXT EVENING, Honora looked at herself in the full-length mirror. She took a deep breath.

The formal gown she'd had made for her in Naples was simple but pretty. The length was short, as it was still August, and soft pink, with an overlay of beadwork. Her dark hair was in a chignon high on her head, glossy and sleek.

At over eight months pregnant, she felt like a whale, but her husband's eyes still lit up when he came into the bedroom. "You look beautiful, *cara*."

"Thank you." Her cheeks burned hot. Nico looked almost unbearably handsome to her. His powerful body was barely contained by the civilized, perfectly tailored tuxedo.

Reaching into his pocket, he pulled out a fistful of sparkling jewels. "I brought you a gift."

Stepping behind her, he placed a cold necklace of enormous rectangle-cut emeralds over her collarbone. As he attached the clasp, he lowered his head and kissed the crook of her neck, making her shiver with dangerous desire.

"Perfect," he said huskily.

She wondered if he would think her so perfect if he knew whom she'd invited to the ball tonight.

Honora faced him, her heart pounding. After his ultimatum on the yacht, he thought she'd given up the issue of his stepmother. But she could not let him keep going down the path he was on. It could only lead to the destruction of his soul. And hers.

Last night, after they'd returned to the villa, he'd kissed her with such sweet tenderness, stroking her body so slowly, so gently, taking his time, so when he'd finally brought her to aching fulfillment, she almost couldn't bear the intensity of her own joy.

But even then, beneath it all, she'd known she still had to stand up for what was right. She couldn't remain silently, passively married to a man who was so intent on destroying his own family. After all, if Nico couldn't forgive the stepmother who'd once been too lost in her own pain to do the right thing, how could Honora expect anything but the same for her and the baby—that they'd be punished or exiled for the slightest transgression?

Either you're with me, or you're against me. You must choose.

She was married to him, pregnant with his baby. She was in love with him. She was on Nico's side. Of course she was.

But sometimes, being on someone's side had to mean being able to tell them when they were wrong. Even if it made them angry. Even if it caused trouble.

If you don't like something, don't suffer in silence, he'd told her. *Be honest. Speak up.*

And that had just been about a plate of sautéed mushrooms. This was about the rest of their lives.

But she was afraid. More afraid than she'd ever been in her life. Inviting Egidia was a huge risk. Honora knew that if Nico could just see her, talk to her in person, they would finally reconcile. He would either forgive her and be glad, or—

Or he wouldn't.

"Nico." She swallowed hard. "There's something you should…"

"Yes?" He looked down at her expectantly.

Her courage failed her. She looked down, putting her hand on the cool, hard emeralds at her throat. "They're beautiful. You didn't have to do this."

"Of course I did. They match your eyes, and you deserve every luxury." Leaning forward, he whispered wickedly against her skin, "Especially after last night."

Her blush deepened as she remembered the previous night's passion. Every night of their honeymoon he'd found new ways to give her intoxicating pleasure.

She just prayed Nico would forgive her for the public ambush, and eventually understand why she'd had no choice but to do this, to make him face the past he'd gone to such lengths to avoid…

"Are you ready?" Nico murmured, holding out his arm.

"I hope so." Nervously, she took his arm. Would he still smile at her so warmly when the night was over?

Together, they left the master bedroom and went down the sweeping staircase of the Amalfi Coast villa as guests began to arrive.

They greeted each guest in the foyer, beneath the soaring crystal chandelier high overhead, and above it, the frescoes of cherubs. But there was no sign of Egidia. Honora felt more and more nervous as the minutes ticked by.

Nico seemed proud to introduce her to his glamorous European friends, many of whom were from Rome or farther away still—Milan, Paris, Athens. For once, Honora had no energy to feel insecure when she met the extravagantly thin, gorgeously dressed supermodels and heiresses and female tycoons. She was too anxious about the coming confrontation to care what strangers thought of her.

The villa's ballroom was as exquisite as a jewel box, filled with flowers, and a string quartet was playing music. Holding a crystal flute of sparkling water, Honora stood beside her husband as he spoke to a small group of people, switching from Italian to English for her sake. She tried to smile and nod and appear as if she were interested in their discussion, which was apparently about some land deal in Malaysia. She felt Nico's hand stroking her bare upper back. Her shoulders felt tense. Her gaze kept straying to the door.

Then she gave an intake of breath.

Nico noticed at once. He looked down at her with a bewildered frown. Then he followed her gaze. His body stiffened.

"What the hell—" His voice choked off in a strangled gasp as he saw the new guest in the ballroom's doorway.

"Forgive me," Honora said quietly. "I had no choice."

An elderly white-haired woman, round and slightly

stooped, dressed in a formal gown that looked like couture, though it was two decades out of fashion, entered the room. Principessa Egidia Caracciola.

Nico's head was spinning.

For the last twenty-four hours, he'd been congratulating himself that he'd convinced his wife to stop fighting for his enemy, aka his stepmother, and to keep her loyalty where it belonged, with Nico. He'd tried to bind her to him more thoroughly, making love to her last night with agonizing slow gentleness—though it damn near killed him to go slow—and buying her an emerald necklace worth half a million euros, which had once belonged to a tsarina of Russia.

He'd introduced her to the cream of European society, which he'd bulldozed into with his wealth, power and charm. He wouldn't call them all friends, exactly, but they were entertaining, and useful, and anyway, it gave him satisfaction to think he'd earned his way into the aristocratic circle his father had tried to deny him.

For the last hour, he'd watched Honora, in her sparkling pale pink cocktail dress, her green eyes brighter than the emeralds at her throat, hold her own against them all, talking easily to even the most arrogant Milanese heiress. His heart had burst with pride for his beautiful, clever, kind wife.

Nico had started to relax again. Maybe he'd overreacted. Maybe he could still trust her. Maybe he didn't need to permanently be on his guard.

And now…this ambush!

He pulled Honora to the side. His jaw was tight.

"Is this about revenge?" he said in a low voice, for her alone. "Is that why you invited her here? To win the argument? To hurt me?"

Honora's forehead furrowed.

"No, Nico," she said, looking bewildered. "I'm trying to help you make peace with your family. With yourself—"

"Peace!" He'd never heard anything more ridiculous. He felt like his heart was about to explode. He couldn't believe she would attack him like this, in such an underhanded fashion, trying to humiliate him in front of European society! What had he ever done to deserve this? Nothing! All he'd ever done was treat her like a queen!

With an intake of breath, he turned back to the grand doorway of the ballroom. Egidia Caracciola. His dead father's widow.

Their eyes met, and his whole body was engulfed in ice.

The ballroom seemed to fall silent, first the guests, then the musicians discordantly cutting off midsong. Nico knew there'd been gossip about the lengths he'd gone to, gathering up Prince Arnaldo's debts, then trying to force the sale of the Villa Caracciola. There had been commentary about the physical resemblance between the two men. Gossiping about secret parentage was always an enjoyable pastime for the jet set, but he'd thought he'd quashed that rumor. Now, he could feel new whispers building around him like wildfire.

"What have you done?" he said hoarsely.

"Please, Nico." Honora's lovely face looked scared.

"Just give her a chance. I'm trying to help you. I love you."

Help. Yes, help him into public humiliation. *Love.* Love him into an early grave. He felt his chest tighten and squeeze and suddenly remembered how his father had keeled over of a heart attack last Christmas without warning.

You killed him! his stepmother had screamed at Nico at the funeral. *I hope you're proud of what you've done, you awful, awful boy!*

And now they were facing each other in person for only the third time in their lives. The first time had been on a street in Rome, when he was seven years old. His mother had pushed him forward, both of them hungry, and he'd been wearing clothes that were too small.

Please, Arnaldo, this is your son. Help us.

His stepmother, wearing her sleek designer clothes, had grabbed his father's arm and gasped, *No. I can't bear it. Tell me it's a lie.*

His father had said coldly, *It's a lie.*

Tension pulsed through Nico's body as he faced his stepmother. This was supposed to be a party. A celebration. Around the elegant ballroom, all his so-called friends, men in tuxedos and the women in shimmering gowns, were watching and listening with interest, the better to gossip about later.

He had to pull it together.

With an intake of breath, Nico walked forward, his traitorous wife trailing behind him. His guests parted, creating a path between him and the elderly Italian woman.

He stopped in front of her.

"Buonasera, signora," he said with a coolly courteous nod. "Welcome to my home."

Lifting her chin, his stepmother replied in the same cool tone, "Thank you for inviting me."

But you weren't invited, Nico raged inside. He forced himself to smile, to take his wife's hand. "We are so glad you could come."

Egidia stood in front of him in her dated gown, her white hair carefully done, and her bright coral lipstick not quite straight on her feathered lips. She drew herself to her full height, which wasn't much, and looked at him, her forehead creased.

Then she sucked in her breath. Her eyes roamed his face, then filled with tears.

"You do look like him," she whispered. "I didn't want to believe it. But you look like Arnaldo when he was young." Her wrinkled face crumpled, as if she were about to cry. "All this time I never realized…" She choked out, "Villa Caracciola should be yours. I will no longer fight it. You are his son. *You are.*"

The old lady moved forward, as if to embrace him. Nico tried to step back, holding up his flute of sparkling water like a shield. But it was not enough.

"Which means…" Lifting up on her tiptoes, she threw her arms around him with a sob. "You are mine…"

Gasps and exclamations rippled through the crowd. Some of the guests had tears in their eyes, obviously enjoying the scene, as if it were some melodrama on television, the reprobate prodigal son being welcomed with open arms by his dead father's widow.

Looking around him, at the way his party had been taken hostage, and his whole life story revealed to people who might somehow use it against him someday, Nico tried to smile and pretend he was calm and pleased. But inside, he was seething with rage greater than he'd ever known. He felt embarrassed, angry, ashamed.

And looking at his beaming wife beside him—so beautiful, *so deceitful*—he knew just who was to blame.

CHAPTER TWELVE

AGAINST ALL ODDS, she'd succeeded.

As Honora watched her husband and his elderly step-mother embrace, tears filled her eyes.

She'd taken a terrifying gamble, inviting the woman here, praying that he could finally forgive her and let go of the resentment and anger poisoning his soul. She'd been so scared that Nico would refuse, that he'd make a scene and toss Egidia from the house, and that he would hate Honora for what she'd done. But she'd been brave enough to risk it anyway.

And this was her reward.

"I'll tell my lawyers the Villa Caracciola should be yours," Egidia Caracciola said tearfully.

"Thank you," Nico said. Looking around at his guests, he added, "I will, of course, pay you the estate's full value."

"That's not necessary—"

"I insist." All the guests smiled approvingly at this obvious generosity, of each side making a concession, the picture of family compromise and unity.

Coming forward, Honora embraced her stepmother-in-law. "I'm so happy," she whispered. "For both of you."

"Me too." The white-haired woman smiled at her through her tears. "All this time I was fighting him, I thought I was protecting my husband's memory. But I was wrong. Nicolo is actually his son. He is the one I must protect now."

Honora glanced at Nico to see if he'd heard. He was watching them, his handsome face impassive. He abruptly gave his stepmother a smile.

"May I get you some champagne?"

For the rest of the evening, Honora felt a warm glow of happiness. After the awful last twenty-four hours, she felt like everything would be all right. Their family was healing. The future was bright—for all of them.

The reception had been a greater success than she'd dared to hope, and she was grateful to all his friends who'd come to wish them well. By the time the last guest had finally left at around two in the morning, trailing off into the cool August night beneath a black sky swept with stars, Honora had spoken with every single person who'd attended. From the Milanese automobile heiress—she was actually very sweet—to the pompous duke with dyed black hair—he told such funny jokes—and thought they were all lovely, lovely people. Honora was happy to call them friends.

As the door finally closed on the last guests, collected by their chauffeurs to head back north to Rome, Honora felt like she'd never been so happy. She turned to face her husband, expecting gratitude, or maybe praise, but not needing either. All she wanted was to share their joy, maybe by him taking her in his arms for a kiss.

But once they were alone, Nico's whole demeanor changed.

"How could you."

His voice was a low growl, his powerful body in the tuxedo standing silhouetted in front of the wide windows facing the sea, bathing him in a pool of silvery moonlight.

Honora didn't understand. She came forward in the pale pink beaded dress, the emerald necklace sparkling coldly against her collarbone. "What do you mean? Everything's better now, isn't it?"

He turned on her, his face coldly furious. "Better?" He let out a low, sharp laugh. "I suppose. At least now I know I can't trust you. Ever. Again."

She felt an icy chill down her spine.

"But the two of you made up," she whispered. "You forgave her. You said—"

"What was I supposed to say, surrounded by guests? Did you expect me to knock the woman down? You knew I could not make a scene. I could not show weakness, or even anger that might reveal how much that woman hurt me."

"But you made peace." Honora felt dizzy. "Egidia accepted you're her husband's son. Even though it clearly hurts her, because it proves that her husband was unfaithful, and also it must make her feel heartbroken about her own babies that died. But she still claimed you. In front of everyone."

He snorted. "Because she knew my lawyers were

at her throat, and she'd soon lose the villa anyway. She thought she could manipulate me, with this *tender family reunion*." He said the words as a sneer. "And it worked. I had no choice but reciprocity. Now I'll be paying her a tidy little bundle, whereas before she would have been left with nothing."

Honora stared at him in horror. "How can you be so cynical?"

"How can you be so gullible? Can't you see how the world really is?"

"Just your own awful world you've created for yourself, where you believe the worst of everyone!"

"And they so rarely disappoint me." Nico's eyes were as cold as a wintry midnight sea. "I should have known you would be the same."

Honora felt a sharp ache in her throat.

"I was trying to help you," she whispered. "I wanted you to forgive your stepmother, and your father too, so you wouldn't be so angry all the time." She abruptly looked away. "I thought if I could heal your heart, then maybe you could love us. The baby and me."

Love us. The longing in her voice as she quietly spoke those words seemed to echo in the ballroom. Wishing. *Begging.*

Nico glared at her, then lifted his chin.

"Why shouldn't I be angry?" His voice was dangerously low. "My wife stabbed me in the back."

Standing in the ballroom, shadowy and dark but for the silvery moonlight flooding the six tall windows, Honora felt forlorn, suddenly shivering in her fancy beaded dress. She saw confetti at her feet, which had been tossed earlier by their friends, saw some cake that had been smashed by someone's shoe into the marble floor. The remnants and trash of the party, like the bitter aftertaste of earlier joy, were all around.

The ballroom was starting to spin. She put a hand to her forehead, trying to breathe. "I never meant to… But you seemed glad!"

His cruel, sensual lips curled. "I lied." He narrowed his eyes. "And I'll never trust you again. Never."

Honora stared at him in the harsh, cold silvery-green moonlight.

She felt shaken to the core. He saw her as his enemy now, she realized—all because she'd tried to heal him.

Did Nico really have no love inside his soul? No ability to care for anyone but himself?

What kind of husband would that make him? What kind of father?

Nico Ferraro is a selfish bastard. Benny's words came back to haunt her. *He doesn't care for anyone but himself. And sooner or later he's going to hurt you. A man like that can do nothing else.*

Shivering, Honora wrapped her arms around her baby bump in the sparkly, pretty cocktail dress. "So I'm your enemy now?"

"You ambushed me. Betrayed me."

She lifted her gaze. "And how do you intend to punish me?"

Setting his jaw, Nico turned to a nearby table. He poured himself a drink of Scotch from a nearly empty bottle. He drank a long sip and didn't answer.

She watched him in despair. "I thought you weren't going to drink as long as I was pregnant."

"And I thought you were on my side." He took another sip. "Seems we're both a disappointment."

She had the sudden memory of her parents' arguments when she was a child, as her mother had raged at her father over his drinking, the two of them clashing and blaming each other. Honora had always felt so small, hiding in a corner or outside the doorway.

After one very loud fight when she was nine years old, her mother had taken Honora back to her childhood home. *I never should have married him*, she'd overheard her mother sob late that night in the kitchen. And Granddad, putting his hand on her shoulder, had replied sadly, *You never should have gotten pregnant before you knew what he was.*

He hadn't known Honora was in earshot. But as she'd crept away to her sleeping bag down the hall, she'd known her parents' unhappiness was her fault, because she had been born. Later that night, her mother had found her crying.

She blinked. "I would give anything to see my mother again," she said quietly. "And my father. I understand better now. I wish I could tell them that. And that I'll always love them." She lifted her gaze. "I wonder if that's what you were wanting this whole time, Nico. Not revenge. *Connection.* For your father to acknowledge you. And your stepmother. It was never about the villa. I think you were just trying to get their attention. I think you wanted…to be a family."

He stared at her, aghast. "Are you out of your mind? I hated them. I vowed to destroy them. And I have."

Honora's shoulders slumped.

Feeling like a burden as a child, she'd done everything she could to be loving and kind and giving, even to the point of eating things she didn't like, and doing things she didn't want to do.

But Nico, feeling unloved, had gone the other way. He wanted to punish anyone and everyone. And he would never stop. Never forgive.

"Now I know I can't trust you, I'm not sure how our marriage can succeed." He drank another gulp of Scotch as he looked out toward the dark moon-swept sea. He looked back at her, his face in shadow. "And it must. For the baby."

Honora's hands froze over her belly. She felt the delicate sparkling beadwork, rough beneath her fingertips.

I'm not sure how our marriage can succeed. And it must. For the baby.

She looked down at her baby bump.

Did she want her daughter to spend her whole life feeling as Honora had—that her parents were trapped in a cycle of misery and blame, all for the apparent benefit of their miserable, blamed child?

She had the sudden memory of her mother's beautiful, sad face when she'd found Honora crying that night in her sleeping bag.

Oh, my darling, don't cry. It's my fault, all my fault. We'll go back home tomorrow. Her young, heartbroken mother had started crying too, and hugged her tight.

Just be happy, Honora. Please. Her voice had caught. *You have to be happy. For all of us.*

Honora suddenly looked up.

"It was never my fault," she whispered.

Nico's head turned, and she saw his sudden scowl, edged with silver light. "What do you mean? Of course it was. You're the one who invited her here."

Honora shook her head, lost in her own realization. "My parents made mistakes. They did the best they could. But I was never to blame. I was just a baby." She looked down, her hand resting protectively on her own unborn child. "I'll never do that to you," she whispered. "Never."

"What the hell are you talking about?"

She looked at him in wonder. "My whole life, I've felt like I didn't deserve to be happy, or speak out for the things I wanted." She shook her head. "You helped me learn to stand up for myself."

"And you turned against me."

"I was never against you, Nico," she said quietly. "I'm always on your side, even now, though you can't see it. I love you." She looked down. "But you'll never love me back."

Nico's posture changed. His dark eyes looked haunted.

"Love was never part of our arrangement," he said in a low voice. "But I didn't want to hurt you. I thought if I romanced you, with passion and gifts—"

She gave him a sad smile. "I know."

He set his jaw. "But *trust*, watching each other's back—that's what I expected in our marriage. And you couldn't even uphold your end of the bargain. That's what your so-called *love* is good for."

Standing in the ballroom of this elegant Italian villa, pregnant with a much-desired child, married to a handsome billionaire and draped in jewels, Honora had never felt so sad and alone.

She thought of how her mother had loved her, so much that Bridget had given up her own chance for happiness, for her child's sake.

What would have happened if her mother had left her father that night for good, and never gone back? Could Bridget have learned to be happy? Could her father have cleaned up his act? Would they both still be alive today—blessed to live long enough to learn to do better?

Honora suddenly saw her choice clearly.

Would she stay with a man who considered her an enemy if she said he'd made a mistake? Would she teach her daughter to feel like a burden? Teach her that families should be filled with anger and blame, rather than forgiveness and love? Teach her that wives stayed and put up with misery, no matter what?

No, she thought. No.

"You have no love in your heart," she whispered. "Not for me. Not for anyone. No love. No forgiveness. Nothing."

"It's who I am," he said coldly. "You knew that when you married me."

"But I thought—" She took a deep breath. "It doesn't matter. I can't live like this anymore."

His mouth fell open. He quickly recovered. "You

can't leave. Under the terms of the prenup, you'll get almost nothing."

"You think I care about that?" she choked out.

"Everyone cares about money, no matter what they say." His dark eyes glittered. "Money is power, and power is everything."

She gave a laugh that was more like a sob. "Money? Power? It's *love* that matters, Nico. Loving your family, but also loving yourself. It's about being kind and helping each other. Because living can be hard, and everyone has secret bruises and broken hearts they try to hide."

Nico looked at her coldly. "I don't."

Honora stared at him. The pain in her throat felt radioactive. "I realize that now. Nothing I can do will help you or heal you. Because you don't want to be helped. You don't want to be healed."

His dark eyebrows lowered. He walked toward her, and his handsome face came fully into the moonlight. He looked younger than he was. His expression seemed strangely lost.

"You can't leave." His voice was uncertain.

"I have to," she whispered, "or you'll drag me into your darkness. Drag all of us."

Stiffening, he glared at her. "Just because I protect myself and don't forgive my enemies. Just because I seek justice. Just because I'm angry you went behind my back and—"

She held up her hand, stopping him midtirade. She felt tired and so, so sad. "Maybe I shouldn't have done it. But I can't let you ruin my life—and our daughter's."

"Our daughter!" He drew back, his expression shocked. "I would never do anything to hurt her!"

Honora took a deep breath, fighting to be reasonable and kind when she felt so hurt. "If that's true, you can still be her father."

"Big of you," he said, sneering.

"I'll make sure she knows you never abandoned her. You can visit her anytime you like. I'll wait until after she's born before I start divorce proceedings."

Nico's voice caught. *"Divorce?"*

She looked at him quickly. His darkly handsome face was as inscrutable as ever. She must have imagined emotion in his voice. He would never feel anything, certainly not hurt, let alone despair.

"I won't ask for alimony. I'll take all the blame," she said. "She'll live with me, but legally, we'll share custody. As long as you're good to her. And don't turn her into your enemy, and try to punish her, or push her utterly out of your life any time she disappoints you."

"You really think I would do that?" he whispered.

Honora took a deep breath, blinking back tears.

"It's what you do," she said.

Turning, she left the ballroom. She was proud of herself that she didn't fall apart, but walked away steadily, without looking back. Pride was all she had to hold on to, and a quiet, desperate hope that someday, somehow, she might climb out of this misery.

I have to stand up for what is right, she repeated to herself desperately, her hands clenched. *To truly love my daughter, I also have to love myself.*

But it was hard for her to even imagine ever being

happy, as she left the only man she'd ever loved behind, in the dark, forlorn ballroom where, just hours before, she'd thought they had a future ahead of them of limitless joy.

Nico had never imagined she'd just *leave*.

The villa was dark as he stood in the ballroom. A few minutes later, he heard her final footsteps and the slam of the front door. It crossed his mind to worry about how she would travel, whether she'd be safe. He paced, then called his security chief, who was staying in the carriage house. "My wife is heading for the garage. Take her anywhere she wants to go. Wake the pilot if necessary. Just go with her, Frank. Keep her safe."

But as Nico hung up, his lips twisted bitterly. Why was he worried about her? In the short month that they'd lived here, Honora had made friends everywhere, both inside this house and in the surrounding villages. She would be safe. Everyone loved Honora, because she loved everyone first.

And she'd said she loved *him*. He'd thought he could trust her, that their marriage would last through anger and arguments and pain. He'd never imagined she'd just…disappear.

Or maybe he had. Nico took a deep breath. Some part of him, deep inside, had always been afraid to fully trust her. He'd known he'd always be on the outside, even of his own family.

Nico carefully set down the glass of Scotch. He'd drunk very little—it had been mostly for show, to prove to her that he could defy her, too. Perhaps to prove it to them both, after the way she'd humiliated him in front of their guests.

I was trying to help you. I wanted you to forgive your stepmother, and your father too, so you wouldn't be so angry all the time. I thought if I could heal your heart, then maybe you could love us. The baby and me.

Feeling numb, he pushed the thought away. He slowly walked through the wreckage of the ballroom, with the mess of food, dropped napkins, used plates, colorful confetti and the pile of brightly wrapped wedding gifts. Gifts. How he hated gifts! As if an emerald necklace could ever make a difference, could make her stay!

Grabbing one wedding present wrapped in silvery sparkly paper with a big bow, he turned and smashed it against the wall. Whatever was inside broke into a thousand chiming shards, like crystal.

It didn't make him feel better. Neither did the early phone call he got a few hours later, as he was trying and failing to sleep in the big bed alone.

"I just got a phone call from Egidia Caracciola's lawyer," his head lawyer told him happily. "I don't know what you did, but she apparently left him a message late last night, as she was leaving your party. She'll be coming into his office this afternoon to sign the papers, transferring the Villa Caracciola to you, free and clear. She's not even asking for payment."

"Pay her the full market value," Nico said tightly.

"But it's not necessary—"

"Do it," he said, and hung up.

Dawn was rising over the eastern horizon, soft and pink. Nico felt restless, trapped in the villa, especially as the villa's staff began arriving to tidy up from the night before.

He longed to go for a run, but the Amalfi Coast was rocky and steep, not like the flat shoreline of the Hamptons. Hiking the cliffs and mountains, with their gorgeous view of the sea for miles, would have to do.

Pulling on a T-shirt and shorts and running shoes, he pushed himself as fast as he could, climbing and descending the rocky path, watching the ground so he did not stumble and fall off the edge to his death. His mind was carefully blank of everything but survival.

He went five miles, brutally pushing himself into the mountains as the sun climbed the wide Italian sky. When he reached the top, he looked back at the vast blue sea. The world was fresh and new and he'd never felt so worn-out and old.

Had she ever been his to lose?

I love you, Nico.

He could still remember how her eyes had glowed so dreamily when she'd first spoken the words. And the way her light had faded in his weeks of silence, as he'd never said the words back to her. How could he, when he didn't know what love was? When his heart was stone?

Honora deserved better. Both she and their baby deserved more than a man who had nothing to offer except cold, hard cash.

A noise came from the back of his throat, and he suddenly stumbled over the steep rocky path. Looking down the rocky slope toward Trevello, he saw his father's ancestral villa, the one he'd wanted for so long, and fought so hard to possess.

I wonder if that's what you were wanting this whole time, Nico. Not revenge. Connection. *For your father to acknowledge you. And your stepmother. It was never about the villa. I think you were just trying to get their attention. I think you wanted to be a family.*

No. Ridiculous. He clawed through his hair. What kind of feeble thing would that be, for Nico to still be trying to get the attention of the people who'd hurt and abandoned him as a child? No. He wasn't that weak or spineless. He'd done it purely for vengeance.

And now he had it. His stepmother was giving the villa to him, as a gift. Last night, she'd publicly acknowledged him as her deceased husband's son.

But looking at the Villa Caracciola clinging to the cliff, Nico didn't feel the happiness and pride he'd craved. Setting his jaw, he descended to the villa's gate.

The door was dangling open. Apparently Egidia Caracciola had already left. It was empty.

As empty as he felt.

His shoulders hurt. He felt bone-weary. And something more. Something he'd spent his whole life trying not to feel.

He felt sad.

But as he started to turn away, he heard a noise. Peeking past the gate, he saw the elderly widow collapsed across the steep, crooked stone steps. She was still wearing her ball gown from last night.

Was she dead?

With an intake of breath, Nico rushed forward. He only exhaled again when he discovered she was, in fact, still alive.

Seeing him, Egidia whimpered, "My leg... I think it's broken."

He reached for his phone, only to remember he hadn't brought it on his hike. "I'll go get help."

"No, please, don't leave me." Her voice was a quiet sob. "I've been out here all night. I thought I would die alone..."

"Where's your phone?"

She gestured wildly to a dense thicket of trees farther down the treacherous hill. "Somewhere—over there—I think," she gasped. "After I tripped, I couldn't find it. I...tried."

Her breathing was uneven, her voice weak with her cheek pressed down against the stone. Nico felt a surge of worry. He kept his voice calm. "I'll find it. What does it look like?"

"It's silver, a clutch bag."

He strode to the copse of trees, looking around with a swiftly pointed gaze, and soon found the 1990s-style bag and the barely more modern phone tucked inside it. Turning it on, he immediately phoned for medical assistance. Then he returned to kneel beside her.

"The ambulance is on the way. Everything's going to be fine," he said gently. "Can I help you get more comfortable?"

Egidia's face was filled with pain and panic, but she nodded. He slowly helped her turn over, so her face wasn't pressed into the stone steps. He flinched when he saw her fractured leg bone, stretching her skin. Following his gaze, she tried to laugh.

"Serves me right. I should have sold you this villa

last year, after Arnaldo died. The truth is, the stairs are too much for me."

She said the words lightly, but he saw the beads of sweat on her forehead.

"I'm sorry I made you fight so hard," he said quietly. "I wasn't nice."

She looked at him quickly. "Neither was I." Her breathing came quick and shallow. "It was hard for me to admit that my husband had a baby with the maid while I was still mourning all the sons we'd lost."

"Honora—" Nico's throat closed around her name "—told me how you've suffered."

Her rheumy eyes filled with tears. "Three little boys. Two lost before birth. The other died before he was a month old. All had the same genetic disorder. After that, we made sure to have no more children. And then…" She looked down. "Then your mother ambushed us on the street in Rome. She pushed you forward, a sweet, dark-haired boy, and said Arnaldo was your father. He told me it was a lie, that your mother was just trying to get money. I wanted so desperately to believe him." She grasped his hand. "And you are the one who suffered for it. I'm sorry."

Nico felt a strange tightness in his chest. "So it wasn't because I seemed unworthy? Useless?"

"Unworthy?" she gasped. "I looked at you on the street, this proud, black-eyed boy, and I wanted so badly for you to be mine. I would have done anything. All I could think of was how my own body had betrayed me, and would not give me what I wanted so badly." She swallowed. "I couldn't see past my own pain. And Arnaldo…he must have been ashamed."

Nico stared at her.

"It was never about me, was it?" he said slowly. She shook her head.

"You were an innocent child, caught up in the lies of adults. When I saw you last night, I was finally forced to admit you were his. And I hated myself for letting my own insecurities and grief keep me from loving you long ago. As every child should be loved." She tried to smile. "You are the brother of the sons I lost."

In the distance, he could hear the siren of the coming ambulance. In the rhythm of the sound, he heard Honora's voice: *My parents made mistakes. They did the best they could. But I was never to blame. I was just a baby.*

"Please, forgive me," Egidia gasped as the paramedics hurried past the gate toward them. Looking down at her, his injured, elderly stepmother, who'd spent the entire night stretched out on cold stone steps, alone and scared, he put his hand gently on her shoulder.

"Only if you'll forgive me, too."

With a sob, she whispered, "Bless you." The paramedics stabilized her leg and loaded her carefully on the stretcher. "And your sweet wife…"

"I'll call the hospital later to make sure you're all right," was the best he could manage. But as he watched the ambulance depart, his heart felt strange.

It felt…lighter.

After all these years of being numb, of priding himself on his hard heart, he watched the ambulance disappear up the narrow cobblestoned street and felt like a burden had suddenly been lifted. Not completely, but just enough for him to be made aware of how heavy it had been all along.

He'd thought his father and stepmother had made some judgment about him when he was a child, that they had found him lacking. But their reasons for rejecting him had had nothing to do with him. They'd been dealing with struggles of their own.

Was it possible that all the times he'd felt ignored, unwanted, an outsider in his own home, it hadn't been about him at all, but about other people's insecurities and pain? His father's shame? His stepmother's anguish? His mother's poverty and heartbreak?

Had Honora been right? All this time he'd thought he wanted revenge, had he really just been hungering for connection, to know his place in the world, to be recognized and seen?

He'd always believed that emotions were a sign of weakness. Anger was all he'd allowed himself. Was it possible that being courageous enough to feel joy, sadness and everything in between was the biggest strength of all?

It's love *that matters, Nico. Loving your family, but also loving yourself.*

Honora's sweetness, her kindness, her passion…all the times she'd sacrificed so much, and risked even more, in her amazing determination to make Nico happy, to make him *whole*—

His heart was pounding. He felt overwhelmed with emotion. All around him, soft golden sunlight seemed to glow over the village of Trevello with a kind of magic as he thought of her. He could almost imagine her on this street, helping Egidia with her groceries, walking the housekeeper's little white dog, talking to everyone, smiling and kind...

Nico sucked in his breath.

He loved her, he realized. He was totally and completely in love.

This was what love meant. Honora was his *family*. His other half, his better half. He needed her. He would die without her.

With a sharp intake of breath, Nico turned and ran up the hillside. He had to talk to her. Now.

Reaching his villa, he threw himself into a cold shower to wash off the sweat. Pulling on a shirt and trousers, he remembered his private plane was still in New York. Grabbing his phone, he saw he'd gotten a text from Frank Bauer to say that Honora had arrived safely, and he'd dropped her off at her grandfather's apartment at her request.

Dialing a number, Nico told his assistant to charter a jet to New York immediately. After he hung up, he stared at the phone, trying to work up the nerve to call Honora. He yearned to tell her everything. To throw himself on her mercy and beg for another chance.

But what if she said no? What if she said he'd hurt her so badly that she couldn't love him again? His hand shook as he hesitated. Being in love was terrifying. She held his life in her hands.

I hope you fall in love with her, Nico. Wildly and desperately. Lana Lee's vindictive words floated back to him. *And I hope you'll suffer for the rest of your life when she never, ever loves you back.*

His phone suddenly rang in his palm, making him jump. The number on screen belonged to Honora's grandfather, Patrick. He snatched it to his ear.

His former gardener's voice was terse. "Honora's in labor. We're at the hospital. She wanted me to let you know. And to tell you that everything is fine."

Even now, Honora was worried about his feelings? His heart was pounding. "*Is* everything fine?"

Silence fell at the other end, then the old man said, "Look, I don't know what you did to her... She says she doesn't want you here." He paused. "But you should come."

"Why are you telling me that? Going against her wishes?"

"Because, well, damn it, you're family."

And he hung up.

Nico stared at the dead phone in his hand.

You're family.

Those simple words cleared out the cobwebs of his mind, exploding the stone walls around his heart, making everything very clear.

Honora was in labor with his baby. Possibly too early. Possibly dangerously so. Terror looped through him.

Grabbing his passport and wallet, Nico ran to the garage. Jumping into the closest car, he started it with a roar, pressing on the gas, heading to the airport where the charter waited, praying he wasn't too late.

Whatever happened, he had to be there. To take care of them. To show them he lived for them. That he'd die for them.

He loved them.

CHAPTER THIRTEEN

IT WAS TOO early for labor. Three weeks too early.

Honora's heart was pounding erratically as she sat in the hospital bed in Queens, in counterpoint to the rat-a-tat of her grandfather's leather soles as he paced by the window. No matter how many times the doctor and nurses had reassured her that her baby's heartbeat seemed healthy and strong, and that the labor hadn't been caused by anything she'd done, she was scared.

She'd been on Nico's private plane crossing the Atlantic when she'd first felt contractions. Could the elevation change or pressurized cabin have somehow set off labor? Or had it been caused by the anguish of leaving the only man she'd ever loved?

"Please, baby," she whispered, her hand on her belly. "Please be all right."

"Don't you worry," Granddad said gruffly, stopping his pacing. "Everything is going to be fine."

She felt a catch in her throat. "What if it's not?"

"Your doctor seems like a pretty smart lady, and she said babies come early all the time." He gave a rueful smile. "They say the baby's lungs should be fine, and if there's any problem, they can scoop her up and take her straight to the NICU... Aw, Honora! Don't do that!"

She'd burst into tears. Sitting on the edge of the bed, he patted her hand. "It'll be all right...you'll see."

"But it's my fault..."

He looked astonished. "How?"

Honora looked up at him miserably. "I have been too upset. I've been crying for hours—and I was on a plane. I should have known better. After everything Mom and Dad went through, I shouldn't have married him when I knew he couldn't love me!"

"Stop right there." His hand tightened over hers. "If anyone's to blame for your parents' marriage, it was me. I shamed your mother into marrying him, and hoped he'd grow into his responsibility. But it didn't turn out, though they both tried. And then—" he blinked fast "—I did the same to you. Hauling my hunting rifle over to Nico's beach house like an old fool."

She stared at him in astonishment. Was her grandfather...crying?

"I'm so sorry, Honora," he whispered. "I never should have done that. I should have listened to you. Trusted you to figure out what was right." He gave a tremulous smile. "I'm sorry."

Shocked, she put her hand on his shoulder. "You were trying to help." Thinking of how she'd tried to help Nico, she looked down. "But sometimes you can't help. Sometimes there's nothing you can do, except love someone from a distance."

Looking up, he said, "You're right. How did you get to be wiser than me?" He tried to smile. "You've always had such a big heart. So eager to help everyone. You love people more than they deserve. Me most of all." He looked up, his eyes full of tears. "I'm so proud of you, Honora. You should know that. How much I…love you."

She couldn't have been more shocked if he'd taken off his boot and thrown it at her.

"You…" Her throat closed.

His eyes were watery. "I never was good at saying that, was I? Or showing it. But I've always loved you, kid."

Her grandfather loved her. The thought was like a warm hug. He hadn't just been taking care of her out of his sense of duty. She'd never been a burden. He loved her.

"I love you too," she choked out, and he hugged her.

Patrick drew back, smiling. "Now, I'm about to meet my new great-grandbaby, who I already know is going to be the brightest, feistiest, most loving child. Just like her mother." His green eyes, so much like her own, glowed beneath his bushy gray eyebrows. "And if that husband of yours can't see what he's missing, he doesn't deserve either of you."

A sudden longing for Nico went through her heart. As she sat in the hospital room, she looked out the window. Outside, it was twilight. Fading red light slanted through the half-open blinds over the sterile equipment and easy-wash floor.

"Oh," she choked out, tensing as she felt a new labor pain start to rise.

As Honora started to gasp with pain, her grandfather rose quickly to his feet. "I'll get the doctor, tell her you want an epidural after all—"

"It's too late," she panted. "They said it's too late." She gasped another breath. "I can handle it—"

And suddenly she knew she could. After all the hard things she'd done in her life, she now knew she was tough and brave enough to handle anything. It was love that made her strong. Love for her baby. Love for her grandfather.

Love for herself.

But she couldn't stop wishing if only Nico could have been part of their lives! If only he'd been able to open his heart!

She would go on without him, living in her old bedroom of her grandfather and Phyllis's apartment, until she graduated from college and could afford one of her own. But it wasn't the life she'd wanted.

If Nico had given her the chance, she would have tried to mend his heart. In a strange way, loving him had helped her mend her own. She would have given anything—

She gasped as her body shook with pain. Her hand tightened on her grandfather's, making him flinch. But she couldn't loosen her grip as the agony built, worse than anything she'd ever known, overwhelming her until she cried out.

"Doctor!" her grandfather shouted. "Nurse!" Pulling away, he rushed to the door in a panic. "Please, someone, my granddaughter needs *help*—"

And suddenly, in the corner of her hazy vision, she saw a large, dark figure push into the room. Not a doctor. Not a nurse.

"Cara."

Honora looked up with a gasp.

Was she hallucinating?

Like a miracle, she saw her husband. He rushed to her bedside, and she saw that his clothes were wrinkled, his jaw unshaven, and he had deep hollows beneath his eyes. But as he leaned forward to take her hand, his dark eyes glowed.

"I'm sorry I'm late. Oh, my darling," he whispered, kissing her sweaty temple. "I'm so sorry."

"What are you doing here?" she choked out. "I told you we're through—"

But even as she spoke the words, she gripped his hand desperately.

"I'm here now." Nico glanced back at her grandfather. "I'm here for her."

Clearly relieved, Granddad nodded, then hurried to join Phyllis in the waiting room.

"You don't know what you're—" Honora began, but then couldn't speak anymore against the flood of pain.

Her husband didn't flinch, no matter how hard her grip became. He didn't look away. He looked straight into her eyes, letting her crush his finger bones without giving the slightest evidence it hurt him. He seemed unbreakable, and as she closed her eyes, lost in pain, she could dimly hear his low voice, telling her how powerful she was, that he was in awe of her strength, that she was an amazing woman, an incredible mother. That he loved her.

As the pain slowly ebbed, letting her breathe normally again, Honora looked at him.

"What did you just say?"

He smiled, and his dark eyes looked emotional, even tender. "Hello, *cara*."

Honora felt a different sharp pain, this time in her heart. Had he followed her all the way to New York City just to tempt her, to torment her with what she could not have? It had nearly killed her to leave him in Italy, even knowing it was the right thing to do. She would no longer settle for second best. She could not give her life to a man who was incapable of loving her.

So had she imagined his words?

"What—what are you doing here?"

"I finally figured out what present to give you. The only gift you'd ever care about."

He still thought he could buy her? Her rising hope crashed to the floor. "I don't care about presents."

"I never liked them either. Until now. Because I've found something I really, really want to give you." Holding her hand, he came in close.

"My heart," he whispered. "For you and the baby. I want to give you my heart." His eyes had a suspicious gleam as he tried to smile. "The truth is, I already have."

She looked at him in amazement. "You're saying—?"

"I love you, Honora."

She stared at him, stricken, afraid to believe. Then she felt the pain rise again, even worse than before. Again, he held her hand, helping her through it, telling her over and over again how proud he was of her, how he couldn't wait to hold their baby, how much he loved her.

When she could finally breathe again, she said, "Why are you saying this? Just because you don't want to lose me? You said you could never love anyone."

"It was myself I didn't love all these years. You were right. But I've learned the truth now. I spoke with Egidia at her villa—"

"You did?" she gasped.

"And she helped me realize that their rejection was never about *me* at all. It's what you said. Everyone has secret bruises and broken hearts that they try to hide." He paused. "You should know Egidia's in the hospital, too. But don't worry, she's going to be all right. She broke her leg on some steps at her house, but I helped her get an ambulance—"

"You helped her?" The world seemed to be spinning. She felt another pain coming. Already. Too soon.

She squeezed his hand, closing her eyes as she endured the agony, surrendering to it. He held her hand quietly, calm and tender and strong. When the pain finally abated, she exhaled.

"All these years I was so wrong, about everything," Nico said. "I thought being hard and cold and numb was the only way to protect myself." Lifting her hand to his lips, he kissed the knuckles as he whispered, "Then I met you."

She felt another rise in pain. Contractions were coming quicker together now, and harder. "Nico—"

"You've changed my life in every way possible. You've changed me, heart and soul." He looked down at her, his handsome face glowing with intensity. "And I swear that whatever it takes, even if takes the rest of my life, I will find a way to win back your love."

She looked up at him, and then her lips parted in shock. "You're crying."

"Yes." He gave a ragged breath, tried to smile as he ran a hand over his eyes. "I feel everything. And what I feel most of all is how much I love you. How much I *need* you," he whispered. "Please, Honora. Tell me I have a chance to win you back. To be the man you need me to be."

He loved her. He actually loved her. The realization was the sweetest feeling Honora had ever known, even as she gasped with agonizing pain. "I feel like I'm dreaming. I can't believe you're even here."

He didn't flinch as she gripped his hand tight enough to break a bone. "Your grandfather told me to come."

"Behind my back!"

"He said I'm family. Is it true, Honora?" He looked down at her. "Am I your family?"

She looked at him.

"Now and forever. I love you, Nico."

Joy filled his dark eyes as he bent and kissed her forehead, her cheeks. *"Cara..."*

Then the pain took over, and her doctor was suddenly there, and nurses, and her doctor was telling her to push, and the pain was so blinding that Honora thought she might die.

Then, suddenly, the pain was over, and forgotten, as a sweet little baby girl was placed in her arms, and her husband wrapped his powerful arms around them both, and all of them were crying.

Many hours later, as Honora held her new daughter, she looked over at Nico. He'd fallen asleep in the hard plastic chair. He had dark circles under his eyes, and scruff over his jawline, and his clothes were wrinkled, and he looked as if he hadn't slept in days. And he'd never been more handsome.

As if he felt her gaze, Nico looked up, then smiled. And the love she saw in his dark eyes filled her heart.

As she held her baby, the dawning sun came in through the window, covering them both with a soft golden glow, and Honora knew that their happiness would always last. They both deserved to be loved. And they'd finally come home to the circle of each other's arms.

The summer sun was bright and hot in the cloudless August sky, as the wild Atlantic waves splashed against the white sand.

Sitting on the grass outside their Hamptons mansion, in the same exact spot where they'd been wed the previous year, Nico looked at the people around him, feeling gratitude and quiet joy.

His wife was snuggled beside him on one of the soft blankets covering the grass, wearing a short, pretty sundress that showed off her slender curves, and a wide-brimmed sun hat. She'd thought of wearing jewelry—nothing fancy, just the golden heart necklace he'd given her for her birthday—but quickly thought better of it the first time baby Kara's hand had wrapped around it and pulled.

No matter. Honora didn't need jewels to make her sparkle brighter than the sun. Nico was dazzled every time he looked at her, as her green eyes glowed and danced while she laughed, her full lips a festive red to match the balloons and streamers.

Their baby sat nearby, wearing a little jumpsuit that revealed the adorable fat rolls at her thighs. She had her mother's green eyes and dark hair. They'd named her Kara, because she was beloved.

Their butler, Sebastian, smiling from ear to ear, had just served sandwiches—tiny ones with the crusts cut off, and fancy cookies with jam, and tea with milk, although their daughter was drinking hers in a sippy cup.

"A tea party?" Nico had asked his wife with amusement. "For a baby's birthday party?"

"Kara likes tea," Honora answered primly, then grinned. "Especially tea with milk."

Now, Nico slowly looked around him at the people who'd somehow become his family.

Honora's grandfather, Patrick, was telling some drawn-out story about the proper raising of lemons, to Egidia, of all people, who'd raised more lemons in Italy than the retired gardener ever had.

His stepmother's leg had completely healed. She no longer had to worry about rickety flights of stairs, as he'd bought her a luxurious single-floor apartment in Rome to live in while her longtime home, the Villa Caracciola, was remodeled and furnished with an elevator. She'd happily accepted Nico's offer to come visit the Hamptons for her granddaughter's birthday. The baby's great-grandmother, Phyllis, was giving Egidia a sympathetic smile, and offering her a cup of Italian espresso and sugar cookies.

His wife's best friend, Emmie Swenson, had arrived in a fluster a few hours before. The two women had laughed and talked together as they'd put up the decorations for the family party, all in red which was Kara's favorite color. Nothing made Honora happier than taking care of people.

Her patience might soon be tested, though, since any minute now, Nico's friend Theo Katrakis was expected for dinner. Which Nico honestly didn't understand.

"Why would *Theo* ever agree to come to a baby's birthday party?"

Smiling at their baby, his wife had crooned, "Because he loves Kara. And she loves her uncle Theo, doesn't she?"

Honora often fretted that his friend didn't have any family to look after him. Nico wasn't worried, but his wife seemed to care about the whole world. It left him in awe. He loved his family, but he couldn't imagine having the capacity to worry about absolutely everyone, not like his wife did.

She'd even been happy to read online that Lana Lee was dating rising star Benny Rossini. "I hope they'll be happy." She'd smiled. "They deserve it."

That was what Nico had learned from her. *Everyone* deserved love. And he knew he'd spend the rest of his life protecting and caring for her—the heart and soul of their family, and beyond.

And so, an hour before, their family had gathered on the grassy bluff overlooking the sand to celebrate their baby's first birthday. The balloons and streamers were hung high in the trees, where Kara couldn't reach them. Nearby, there was a small pile of presents that they'd just helped their daughter unwrap. None of the gifts were expensive. Beach toys, like a bucket and shovel. A truck. A teddy bear. As Honora had taught him, it was about love, not money.

Good thing too, since Kara seemed mostly interested in playing with the discarded wrapping paper.

They were planning to go down to the beach in a bit and make sandcastles, assuming the star of the party didn't try to eat any of the sand. And later tonight, after dinner, when the sun fell softly into the sea, they'd gather around a bonfire on the beach, roast marshmallows and sing songs before Nico carried their sleepy baby against his shoulder, back to the house, to tuck her into her crib.

And then, Nico knew the rest of his family would finally disappear to their rooms, and he could be alone with his wife. He would hold her in his arms, setting fire to the night, as outside their bedroom's open window the summer stars would sweep across the wide sky and the surf would roar against the shore.

He hoped they'd have more children. Five. Six. As many as she wanted—as many as they could handle. What the hell else was money for? He'd just buy a bigger house. A bigger jet. And be ready for a bigger heart.

"What are you thinking?" Sitting beside him on the blanket, Honora looked up at him suspiciously.

Leaning forward, he whispered in her ear, "I want to unwrap you."

He had the satisfaction of seeing his wife blush, feeling her body shiver. Oh, yes. Six children. Tonight would be just the start of the joy that would last all their lives.

Nico remembered how numb and broken he'd felt in

this empty house last summer, and all the gray months before. Then Honora had burst through the door and given him a new dream. A new life.

Now, as Kara toddled nearby and the grandparents laughed at some joke Patrick had just made, Honora suddenly leaned forward and whispered something in his ear.

With an intake of breath, Nico looked back at her, wide-eyed. "Are you sure?"

His wife nodded shyly, glowing with visible happiness. "In February." As he started to gasp and turn towards the others, she whispered, "Don't tell. Let's just keep it between us for now. Our little secret."

His glance dropped briefly to her belly, and he nodded, almost dizzy with happiness.

After years of making big real estate deals, he'd finally found the place that was the hardest to create, and the most precious to hold: a real home. In giving away his heart, he'd gotten back more love than he'd ever thought possible. Love was infinite, he thought, looking out at the wide blue ocean. It never ended.

Nico could hardly remember a time before he loved her. It seemed to him now that he'd loved Honora even before he knew her. They'd been brought together by fate, as she'd once said. And that was the greatest secret of all. The two of them were meant to be.

* * * * *

Swept away by The Italian's Doorstep Surprise?
Why not explore these other stories by Jennie Lucas?

Chosen as the Sheikh's Royal Bride
Christmas Baby for the Greek
Her Boss's One-Night Baby
Claiming the Virgin's Baby
Penniless and Secretly Pregnant

Available now!

WE HOPE YOU ENJOYED
THIS BOOK FROM

⊕ HARLEQUIN

PRESENTS

Escape to exotic locations where passion knows no bounds.

Welcome to the glamorous lives of royals and billionaires, where passion knows no bounds. Be swept into a world of luxury, wealth and exotic locations.

8 NEW BOOKS AVAILABLE EVERY MONTH!

#3941 THE WEDDING NIGHT THEY NEVER HAD
by Jackie Ashenden

As king, Cassius requires a real queen by his side. Not Inara, his wife in name only. But when their unfulfilled desire finally gives her the courage to ask for a true marriage, can Inara be the queen he needs?

#3942 MANHATTAN'S MOST SCANDALOUS REUNION
The Secret Sisters
by Dani Collins

When the paparazzi mistake Nina for a supermodel, she takes refuge in her ex's New York penthouse. Big mistake. She's reminded of just how intensely seductive Reve can be. And how difficult it will be to walk away...again.

#3943 BEAUTY IN THE BILLIONAIRE'S BED
by Louise Fuller

Guarded billionaire Arlo Milburn never expected to find gorgeous stranger Frankie Fox in his bed! While they're stranded on his private island, their intense attraction brings them together... But can it break down his walls entirely?

#3944 THE ONLY KING TO CLAIM HER
The Kings of California
by Millie Adams

Innocent queen Annick knows there are those out there looking to destroy her. Turning to dark-hearted Maximus King is the answer, but she's shocked when he proposes a much more permanent solution—marriage!

HPCNMRB0821